Outstanding Praise for Trevor Scott

"Fa   unch
title   DATE D'   *rarv*
Jou

"Trevor Scott manages another winner with this exciting tale set in the middle of the Cascade mountain range on the Northwest. Scott's background and knowledge of all things relating to bombs puts him in the driver's seat, and the reader is the fortunate recipient of an excellent plot, well-crafted characters, and constant action. He never fails to please."—*Midwest Book Review* on Boom Town

"Global Shot is a deftly written, highly recommended action/adventure suspense novel that will have the reader gripped in total fascination from first page to last with its plot twists and unpredictable developments leading to a memorably vivid conclusion."—*Midwest Book Review*

"Vital Force is the riveting novel of rapidly paced, non-stop, action adventure. The stuff of which block-buster movies are made, Vital Force is very highly recommended reading for those who enjoy a well crafted spy-thriller story."—*Midwest Book Review*

"Author Trevor Scott takes us on a thrill ride full of spy-craft, geo-political espionage, advanced weaponry, treason, and a man's fine appreciation for the female body, even when its owner is a stone killer."—*Jules Brenner, Critical Mystery Tour*

"A damned good writer."—**David Hagberg**, bestselling author of more than 70 mysteries and thrillers.

"*Strong Conviction* is a good crime story with interesting characters and solid writing. Trevor Scott weaves a web of small-town controversy that entraps our hero...with vivid description he paints characters who breathe and sets up believable conflict."—*Pine Bluff* (Arkansas) *Commercial*

"*Strong Conviction*...a first class shocker fully developed with crystalline and lively dialogue, adroit pacing, and commanding characters who find themselves enmeshed in extraordinary and often deadly circumstances, with the right mix of potent romantic interest."—*Scribesworld*

"Mr. Scott brings his powerful and prestigious experience into play with his newest thriller, *Hypershot*. Mr. Scott utilizes his usual arsenal of literary techniques to build *Hypershot* into a first-class thriller: pacing, effective love interests, compelling characters finding themselves in unusual and deadly circumstances, clear and effective dialogue, and just plain thrilling circumstances. His settings are reminiscent of James Bond. A great fourth book!"—*Midwest Book Review*

"Previous titles have fit the Tom Clancy techno mold, but this topical tale of DNA research and a possible cure for heart disease falls more in the James Bond tradition of fancy cars and fast women."—*Publishers Weekly* on *The Dolomite Solution*

"Trevor Scott delivers with *The Dolomite Solution*. Scott ratchets up the action. He is an expert at thoroughly deceiving the reader, drawing us into a seemingly insolvable plot just as he fascinates us with action that is non-stop...a wonderful read."—*Midwest Book Review*

"Scott has the high-tech jargon down pat...he takes readers around the world for a thrill-packed adventure. Technothriller fans looking for an alternative to Clancy will find Scott a somewhat smaller-scale but perhaps even more authentic alternative."—*Booklist* on *Extreme Faction*

"Trevor Scott's action-packed post-Cold War spy thriller is certainly that-a thriller. *Extreme Faction* takes the reader around the world, into different cultures, lifestyles and ideals with flawless ease. I'd recommend this adventure highly."—*Duluth News-Tribune*

"*Extreme Faction* is fast-paced, realistic, and more than a bit frightening."—*Statesman Journal*, Salem, Oregon

"*Extreme Faction* is a thrill-packed, non-stop, absolutely riveting action/adventure, novel from first page to last."
—*Midwest Book Review*

"A great read. A roller coaster ride of murder, espionage and intrigue."—**David Hagberg**, author of *High Flight*

"*Fatal Network* is a masterfully written, splendidly executed, superb thriller."—*Midwest Book Review*

"This is a thriller with some real thrills, an adventure with new ideas, and an espionage drama firmly rooted in the convoluted realities of modern Europe. A real gut-buster of a thriller."—*Statesman Journal*, Salem, Oregon

"Unique twists and turns...a deadly cat and mouse game."
—*Duluth News-Tribune*

Also by Trevor Scott

Rise of the Order
Global Shot
Boom Town
Vital Force
Fatal Network
Extreme Faction
The Dolomite Solution
Hypershot
Strong Conviction
The Dawn of Midnight

BURST

of

SOUND

A Tony Caruso Mystery

Trevor Scott

Broadhead Books
Beaverton, Oregon

BURST OF SOUND
Copyright © 2008 by Trevor Scott

Broadhead Books
P.O. Box 7396
Beaverton, OR 97007

www.salvopress.com

Visit the author online at www.trevorscott.com

Library of Congress Control Number: 2007940198

ISBN: 1-930486-73-1
9781930486737

Printed in U.S.A.
First Edition

For Paula

Acknowledgments

Thanks to the people of Kitsap County, Washington, the setting of this work of fiction. Again, I salute my old Navy buddies in aviation ordnance. When most young men of our age were in college playing drinking games, we were loading bombs on the dark, slippery pitching decks of aircraft carriers—serving our country when it was not cool to do so.

PROLOGUE

Fifteen Years Ago

The Navy SH-60 Seahawk helicopter cruised along a hundred feet above the raging Indian Ocean at close to its maximum speed of 180 knots, the swirling winds shoving the two-man flight crew around the cockpit like dice in a shaker. In the back, strapped into mesh seats, the two naval officers, dressed in jungle fatigues with no insignia and no rank, held onto straps as the helo took a sudden drop from turbulence.

Lieutenant Tony Caruso grasped the mesh seat and tried not to lose his evening chow. Such as it was. Calcified hockey puck hamburgers and cold, shriveled French fries. At least the coffee had been strong and hot, but even that seemed to be sloshing around in his gut now. High winds and heavy seas my ass, Tony thought. More like a frickin' typhoon. But he knew that the turbulent ride wasn't the only thing upsetting his stomach. It was the nature of this mission. A screw-up of epic proportions. And now he and his buddy Caleb would have to clean up after those jet jockeys.

Tony glanced at his friend, Lieutenant Caleb Hatfield. His eyes were closed behind his goggles, and Tony guessed this was the last place he wanted to be. He hated helos. Damn things didn't have wings. Everything needed wings to fly. These things defied gravity.

Sitting next to Lt. Hatfield, Petty Officer Second Class Brian St. Ours, a flight engineer, looked half asleep. Earlier he had told Tony he was used to picking up strange folks under strange circumstances for uncertain reasons. This had been no exception. Six hours ago they had been summoned to the ready room of their aircraft carrier, the USS Enterprise, for a mission briefing. A few hours ago they had strapped into the helo and taken off into the darkness. They had been escorted for the first hour and a half by an S3 Viking configured as a tanker. They had taken a long drink to extend their range and departed alone to the drop point, which they should have been approaching soon.

The chopper lurched with a gust, dropping at least twenty feet in a couple seconds.

Tony held on to his mesh seat and Caleb almost fell out of his.

"That's normal, sir," Petty Officer St. Ours yelled to both men. "Weather said we'd run into this shit. Think of it as a roller coaster ride. No charge." He smiled broadly, his cheek bones pushing up against his flight goggles.

Tony and Caleb were Aviation Ordnance officers from two different A-7E squadrons on their last cruise before shifting to the F/A-18. The Navy ordnance folks were considered the craziest bastards on any carrier, loading anything from 20mm cannons to nuclear bombs onto aircraft on a pitching deck, in the dark and rain. Nobody screwed with ordnance on or off duty. The Red Shirts were notorious liberty hounds, trying their best to drain any port city of their beer supply.

Shifting forward in his seat somewhat, Lt. Caruso caught the petty officer's attention with a wave of his hand. "How much longer?" he yelled.

The petty officer swung his microphone to his mouth and asked the flight crew. He nodded his head and then shifted toward Tony. "Feet dry in five. Drop in ten."

Tony acknowledged with a thumbs up and leaned back in his chair, closing his eyes.

Minutes later the petty officer shouted "feet dry," meaning they were now over land, which was no great comfort to Tony.

Caruso opened his eyes and shoved his elbow into the ribs of his partner. "Let's go, Caleb. Time to earn some beer money."

Lt. Caleb Hatfield smiled as he pulled his backpack closer to his feet. "I could use a beer right now."

"Hey, we take care this shit and they'll give us a week in the P.I.," Caruso yelled.

The petty officer rose from his seat. "Just a few minutes out," he said. "We won't have time to linger. We'll need a drink just to make it back to our boat."

The chopper slowed now and started to lower toward the ground. They would not be able to set down, so the ordnance officers would have to drop down by ropes. Under normal circumstances this would have been no problem for either of them, but, considering the weight of the backpacks, and what was contained within, neither of them was looking forward to the task. Additionally, their briefing had mentioned the rough terrain and the thick jungle, so they had no idea what dangers lay below in the darkness.

"Let's go," Caruso said, standing carefully and swinging the 75-pound pack to his back. He shifted the pack to center the weight, and made sure he could still access his .45 automatic pistol strapped to his right hip. No problem.

The petty officer waved them toward the starboard door, which he slid open now. He helped Lt. Hatfield strap onto the line, and then he hoisted the cord over the side.

In seconds, Hatfield gave a thumbs up and then disappeared over the side into the darkness.

Caruso hitched up, but the petty officer grabbed him by the arm. "Sir, remember. We'll be right at this spot in twenty-four hours to exfiltrate. You must be here on time."

Caruso smiled. "You get your asses here and we'll be waiting for a cold one."

The petty officer patted him on the backpack. Then Caruso swung over the side and lowered himself into nothingness.

Seconds after Caruso hit the ground, after fighting

his way through the thick jungle limbs, the cord rose back up to the chopper. And then, as if it had never been there, the swishing and whirring of blades disappeared into the abyss of night.

The wind picked up and rain plastered the two men.

Caleb, ten feet away, removed his flight deck helmet and replaced it with a jungle boonie hat. Then he pulled out his cabar knife and took a slice from the bark.

By now, Caruso had also replaced his headgear and was checking his compass. "You think those weather weenies could have predicted a damn monsoon."

"Let's go, Boy Scout," Caleb said. "What ever happened to Be Prepared?"

Tony followed his friend through the thick underbrush. "The Scoutmaster didn't say shit about a Java jungle."

The two men reached their target just as the sun started rising over the mountains to the east. Tony peered through his binoculars at the twisted trees and gnarled remains of what had once been huts. At least that's what he thought they were, but it was hard to tell from a hundred yards away.

"This is bullshit, Tony." Caleb whispered.

"Hey, I didn't order us out to this hell hole."

"Why didn't they just come through a second time and finish the job?"

That was the problem and both men knew it, yet neither wanted to speak the truth. To say it out loud meant they would have to live up to whatever they found in that village. Considering the craters and destruction, Tony didn't expect to find much.

Caleb looked through the binoculars for the first time. "Jesus Christ! How could they have been this far off target?"

According to their briefing, the four A-7Es had been exactly 10 miles off on their bombing run. That was one entire island away in the Sunda Islands of Indonesia.

"It was dark," Tony said. "They were under pursuit."

Caleb poked his finger into Tony's chest. "Don't defend those assholes."

"I'm not. We should have hauled their asses out of their cozy staterooms to clean up their own mess."

"Yeah, that would happen. Come on. Let's sanitize this place and get the hell outta Dodge."

The two of them made their way down the embankment, through razor-sharp palmetto fronds, and toward the bombed out area. It didn't take them long to realize what had been reported from the dark air of the jet cockpit at thousands of feet had no direct bearing on reality. Tony stumbled across it first.

"What's this?" Tony said. They were on the outer edge of a crater, with bamboo shards cluttered about at their feet. Tony kicked aside the debris, revealing a dark foot. "Oh, God." The foot wasn't attached to anything.

As the sun shone now across both of their faces, they swiveled their eyes from one spot to the next. Body parts. Torn flesh. Dried blood, soaked from the rains that had just stopped an hour ago. They moved their way deeper into the encampment. Now there were torsos, some intact, some not.

Caleb started to turn around, but Tony grabbed him by the sleeve. "Where you going?" Tony asked, his gaze penetrating his friend's teary eyes.

"Listen, I didn't sign up for this shit," Caleb yelled, pushing Tony's hand away.

"And I did?"

Almost in tears now, Caleb muttered, "There's gotta be fifty people here." Glancing to his right, his eyes settled on an infant child, its eyes open wide as if seeking the beast in the sky that did this. "Oh, Christ. A baby."

Tony covered the child with a few palm fronds and shook his head. He knew that this would never leave him. He could never escape this nightmare. But, somehow, he also knew they had a job to complete. And they had less than twenty-four hours to complete their task.

Caleb was on his knees sobbing now. Tony knelt next to him, put his hand on the man's shoulder. "Caleb, we've gotta move," he whispered into his friend's ear.

Nodding his head, Caleb slowly rose to his feet and wiped away the tears.

Moving about the compound now with purpose, they found what they were looking for. Two of the two-thousand-pound laser guided bombs had somehow failed to explode. They could not allow the unexploded ordnance to remain there for some unsuspecting person to come upon. Who knew what would happen. They could beat on it with a hammer, not knowing the gravity of its contents. Both men knew their real reason for setting off the explosives, though. Yet, neither man spoke it out loud. They were cleaning up a Navy mess that could not stay there. It was evidence of a crime. An accident, yes, but a crime nonetheless. All of those people, simple folks who still lived off the jungle, old men, women, and babies. It was too much to consider.

It took them no time at all to strap the C-4 to the bombs. And it would be overkill, they both knew. All they really had to do was place a small charge on the fuse, which would in turn set off the booster, exploding the bomb in a chain just like normal. But they had used all they had from each backpack. No need to bring any back with them.

When they were done placing the charges, they stepped quietly through the debris field and back toward the hill. From there they could hide behind a berm and set off the charges.

The explosions went off as advertised, sending dirt and tree limbs in all directions, and leaving behind two craters larger than all the others.

Slowly they started walking back toward the exfiltration point, neither saying a word. What they didn't know, until it was too late, was that they were being watched and followed.

CHAPTER 1

Now

Hail pounded the windshield of Tony Caruso's Ford pickup truck, making it almost impossible for him to see the high mountain road in front of him, the wipers flipping faster than his eyes could keep up.

Tony knew that April hailstorms were not rare to the Oregon Cascades, but usually the precipitation came in the form of snow or rain, depending on the elevation. But not this crap.

He had been shooting photos along the upper McKenzie River, where the spring melt churned ice-cold water from the Three Sisters and Mount Washington Wilderness Areas, and eventually ended up in Eugene, combining with the Willamette on its way to the Columbia in Portland.

For the past couple of weeks, he had been staying with his sister Maria in Eugene in her hundred-year-old renovated house near the University of Oregon campus. A professor of psychology, Maria fit in perfectly with the far left coast—a problem for Tony around election time, since he was about as political as a three-year-old. He just didn't care any more. They were all a bunch of self-centered self-serving criminals as far as he was concerned. So he and his sister agreed to disagree, or at least to not talk about anything political. Keep the peace. There was a mutual target for both of them, Maria's former almost husband and likely father of her thirteen-year-old daughter. Jim or John or Joseph. . .whatever his name was, as far as they both knew, was still hugging trees, literally, somewhere in the San Francisco Bay Area. He was a tree sitter, or as Tony liked to call him, a tree shitter, since he had to send his feces down in a bucket. Tony and Maria both tried their best to not mention the guy to Maria's daughter, Amber. But she was a smart kid. She watched Fox News and would catch a story from time-to-time, which usually included the shit bucket. Amber had told Tony just last week that maybe her real dad was really some random doctor or lawyer her mom had fucked. Well. . .she had said "slept with."

When Tony's cell phone jangled, he hesitated before picking up. It was a mystery to him why he just didn't turn off the damn thing when he was out in the mountains, where cell service was sparse. "This better be good," Tony said.

A short pause. "Is this Tony Caruso?" It was a woman, but that's all he could tell.

"Hey, I'm driving right now," Tony said. "Trying to stay alive in a mountain hail storm."

He rounded a corner sharply and felt movement in

the bed of the truck. Glancing in his rearview mirror, he saw his Giant Schnauzer, Panzer, scramble to a sitting position. The dog was protected by a bed topper, but Tony didn't like to shake him like that. He slowed the truck and pulled over to the side of the road after crossing a bridge that passed over the McKenzie River.

"I'm sorry," the woman said. "This is Mary Hatfield."

It was strange that Tony had not recognized her voice, even though it had been a couple of years since he had heard her speak. Mary Hatfield was the wife of his old Navy buddy, Caleb Hatfield.

"Mary. What's wrong?" Her voice sounded sad and tired.

"It's Caleb."

Shit. "Is he all right?"

"That's just it. I don't know. He's missing."

"What you mean, missing?"

"As in not seeing him for almost a week."

Tony thought about that, trying his best to understand what she was saying. "You still live in Port Orchard?" They had retired across the bay from the Bremerton, Washington shipyard.

"Yeah, Tony. Same house."

"Listen. I'm in Oregon. In the mountains. You're breaking up."

"I thought Caleb might be there with you," she said, her voice barely audible, yet hopeful. "Fishing?"

"No. I haven't seen Caleb in two years," Tony said, guilty for not having attended his friend's retirement ceremony a year ago.

"Can you find him for me?" she asked.

Tony thought for a moment, his eyes transfixed on the hail pelting his windshield. "Yes, of course. But it'll take me a while to get there. At least six or seven hours." Maybe more, Tony thought, if the hail kept falling like this. "Make that tomorrow sometime. I've been up in the mountains all day."

"Thanks, Tony. I was on your website, so I know your rates."

"Forget about that, Mary. Caleb's my friend."

He waited for her to respond, but she was crying, or at least trying her best to hold back tears.

She whispered 'thanks' and then hung up.

The hail slowed suddenly and was now only a light dropping of peppercorn. Tony got out and went to the back of the truck, letting his dog out.

The Giant Schnauzer, it's ears erect and its nose to the ground cruising the small parking lot, suddenly stopped and looked directly at Tony, who snapped his fingers. The dog ran to him and sat at his feet.

"Well, Panzer," Tony said. "Looks like we'll be driving to Washington tonight."

♦

Tony had called his sister to say he would be in Washington visiting an old Navy buddy, and she had seemed almost relieved. He guessed Maria and her two cats were sick of Tony's dog, Panzer, terrorizing them with love. Although Panzer could have snapped their necks with a slight collapsing yawn, he usually just licked them into submission. Amber loved Panzer, though, and let him sleep in her room. Maria might have also been relieved, Tony knew, because he had promised to take Amber out to the shooting club to learn how to handle weapons—the object of derision for any true lefty.

Tony had made it as far as Kelso, Washington, along I-5, stayed the night, and got up early the next morning to drive the last leg.

He stopped in Tacoma for an early Chinese lunch, before crossing the Tacoma Narrows Bridge to the Kitsap peninsula.

Now he cruised slowly along the outskirts of Port Orchard. It was a remarkably clear day, considering how Kitsap County can be at times, with torrential rains pounding you into a submissive, depressed angst that only a couple swigs of whisky could make worse. A few miles back he had actually viewed the Olympic Mountains for a microsecond.

He pulled into Commander Caleb Hatfield's driveway, parked his Ford F250, stepped out onto the pavement, and glanced back across to the North. The commander had done well for himself upon retiring, but couldn't quite pull himself away from the Navy. From his house, he had an unobstructed view of Bremerton Harbor, the Naval Shipyard there, and currently three aircraft carriers, which were undoubtedly of most interest to Caleb Hatfield. Tony and Caleb had served together on one of those ships that now sat idle in its mooring there.

"Tony?"

He turned with that familiar call, and viewed

Caleb's wife Mary for the first time in over two years. She approached from the porch of their century-old, Victorian house, her hair somewhat disheveled. She brushed the long blonde locks behind her ears and wiped tears from her eyes in one familiar movement. She was pretty much as Tony had remembered her. Her long legs seemed to move almost mechanically toward him. By any measure she was still quite attractive, her body kept lean by either aerobics or replacing food with drink. Probably the later.

Tony let her do the talking. She gave him a big hug, a kiss on the cheek, and then stepped back to examine him. "Civilian life has been good to you, Tony," she said, trying to smile, but her lips quivering with each word.

He took a nose hit from the cloud of alcohol about her. Vodka, he guessed. "You haven't changed a bit," Tony said, and she would have to decide if that was a compliment.

Her expression changed from bad to worse. "Still a drunk, is that what you mean?"

"No! Of course not. I..."

"I'm kidding," she said, taking his hand. "Let's go inside." She pulled him toward the front door. "Jeez, you used to have a sense of humor."

"Can I let Panzer out?" Tony asked.

She looked back at his truck. "It was a puppy last time I saw him."

Tony opened the truck topper and Panzer jumped out and roamed the yard. "He's grown a little since then."

"He'll be all right. I'll notify the neighbors to bring in their small children."

They went inside and Tony sat on the sofa, while Mary went to the wet bar across the room, poured herself a drink from a bottle of Absolut Vodka, and without even thinking, she poured one for him as well. Then she came to him and, after handing him his drink, plopped down on the sofa next to him without spilling a drop. A pro. She pulled a couple of photo albums across the coffee table. Without saying a word she slowly flipped through them.

Tony had been working in the private sector for a couple of years now. He used his Ford truck as his office, his laptop with a mobile card his research center, and the truck bed a place to sleep in a pinch. However, he had recently finished working a case in Idaho, where he had cleared a case of bombings that had escalated from mail boxes to cattle. Turns out it was a farm kid, a 16-year-old boy, who just wanted to see things blow up. What the hell ever happened to frogs? Most of Tony's cases dealt with investigating explosions of some sort or another, since he had been with Navy Aviation Ordnance before a stint with the FBI bomb unit.

As Mary flipped through the pages, she stopped at a photo taken of two young ensigns leaning against a 500-pound general purpose bomb strapped beneath the wing of an A-7E Corsair. The two of them were smiling broadly, their sunglasses glistening from the waves of the South China Sea. Caleb was a good six inches taller than Tony's five-ten, and his curly blond hair glistened in the bright sunlight. But, whereas

Tony was built wide at the shoulders, Caleb's physique was more angular. Bastard could eat anything and not gain an ounce, Tony thought.

"You were two cuties back then," she said, pointing her finger at the picture.

"Yeah, we're just a couple of old bastards now."

"That's the Tony Caruso that I knew," she said, smacking him across the chest with her backhand. She sighed heavily and seemed to shake like a baby does when it pees its diaper.

"Mary. We need to focus here." He pulled her chin up to look at him. "You said on the phone that Caleb took off. Just up and left. That doesn't sound like the Caleb I know."

She nodded her head. "That's why I called you. You know him. Everything he does is calculated, precise. Damn Navy Ordnance taught him that. Everything had to be perfect."

Tony was wondering if she was talking about his home life as well. Glancing around the house, he noticed that it was spotless. He couldn't find a speck of dust even if he pulled his white gloves out of storage. She was right, though. The one thing that ordnance had instilled in the both of them was precision. The alternative could have gotten both of them killed more than once.

"How long has he been gone?" Tony asked.

"A week."

He shrugged. "That's not a lot of time. Maybe he went up into the mountains fishing." It was April now, and he knew that Caleb loved to fish the mountain streams in the Spring.

"I thought he might have been with you, Tony. I was hoping that he had found you and the two of you were drinking beer, smoking cigars, and bullshitin' about your Navy days." She flipped a couple of pages, stopping on a group of pictures with Caleb, Tony and half a dozen other sailors hoisting beers at the photographer in their favorite bar in the Philippines.

"How has he been the last few weeks?" Tony asked.

"Pretty much the same. I had no clue he would up and leave me here."

"No fights?"

"Not with me. He was bitchin' a lot for the past couple of months. But it had nothing to do with us." Her eyes shifted sideways at him. She was holding something back.

"Listen. I can find him a lot faster if you tell me everything you know."

She picked up her vodka, stood up rather formally, and took a sip with both hands supporting the glass. It seemed like she wanted to bolt herself at this moment, her eyes shifting sideways at him. Finally, she walked over to a small secretary next to the wet bar, shuffled through some papers, picked up a letter, stared at it for a moment, and then walked slowly back toward Tony. Her left hand shook the remains of her vodka, while she gently offered the paper to him.

Tony took the letter and immediately started in. The first thing he noticed was the letterhead, which had been made with some cheap word processing program and printed on a lousy dot-matrix printer.

Damn, he thought all of those printers had been hauled out to sea and dumped to make a fish-habitat reef. The letter was addressed to Caleb Hatfield. No mention of commander or Navy. Just Caleb. It was from the Environmental Defense League, whatever that was. Tony was guessing it had nothing to do with little league baseball or the federal government. There was no signature, no name, only a paragraph of rambling. The writer wanted to thank the reader, and expressed deep concern over the matter they had discussed at their last meeting. Very cryptic. The letter actually looked like a copy of some sort.

He flipped over the letter, scanning for any sign of who might have written it or when it was sent. Nothing.

Tony shrugged. "So, what's this?" he asked Mary.

She took a seat next to him again. "I don't know. Caleb mentioned something about one of his fishing partners bringing along a guy from EDL on their last trip up into the Olympics. He said they had a lot in common, but I never met the guy."

"When was this?"

"Last Fall," she said, trying to rack her brain. "It was in early November, I think."

He looked at the letter again. Something wasn't right about it. He got up and went to the secretary, found another piece of standard letter paper, and compared the two of them. That's what he thought. The EDL letter was a little shorter. And there was a rough edge at the top. Someone had cut the top off.

"Do you have a fax machine, Mary?"

She got up and headed toward him. "Sure. It's in

Caleb's office. Why?"

"I think this came in as a fax. Someone cut the return number off the top, though. Where did you find this?"

"I started looking through his stuff this morning," she said. It was stuck to another piece of paper under a stack of bills in Caleb's office."

Looking at the letter again, he could see a blotch of something on the front.

"I think it's jelly," she said. "He ate a lot of his meals at his desk."

That gave him an idea. He had no clue if this faxed letter had anything to do with anything, but he also knew that he had nothing else to go on. Nothing to indicate why Caleb would leave.

"Could I see Caleb's office?"

Without answering, she led him to an expansive office with bookshelves on two walls. The place looked more like a library, with beautiful wood wainscoting covering textured plaster, and solid hardwood floors polished as bright as the officer's quarterdeck on the USS Enterprise. She left him there, going back down the hall to answer a phone call on another line.

Tony felt somewhat strange sifting through a friend's papers, unsure of what he might be looking for, and equally unsure of what he might do if he found what he suspected he would. First, he found the bill that the fax had been stuck to. He made the assumption that the fax would have come in on the day the fax did, or at least close to it. The bill was a local phone bill, which had been mailed from

Tacoma on the first of April. It would have gotten to him on around the second. That would give him something to go on, but not a helluva lot.

Next he found Caleb's computer and turned it on. While he waited for that to go through the warm up, he examined the fax machine. He got lucky. Caleb had bought state of the art. He sequenced through the memory and finally found what he was looking for. Then he printed a list of all incoming and outgoing calls for the past few months.

When the computer was ready, he started a major search for anything that might help him figure out what Caleb had been up to in the past few weeks. He checked his temp files for both the windows program and those cached from the internet. There wasn't enough time to look at those now, so he saved them all and started uploading them to a server where he had his website hosted. He could check them out later from his laptop when he had time.

"What are you doing?" Mary had returned, a new glass of vodka in her hand and an extra one for him, which Tony accepted.

"I'm sorry. I hope you don't mind. I needed to check out his computer to see what he's been up to in the past few weeks."

"No, not at all. That makes sense. What's that? A fax come in?"

Tony pulled the papers from the fax machine, which had just finished pumping out the last page. "No. These are all the faxes that have come and gone from this machine in the last three months."

She raised her brows with that revelation. "Really?

I had no idea you could do that."

"Only the newer machines," Tony said. Newer? Most fax machines were obsolete, replaced by e-mail and attachments. Only the entrenched dinosaur businesses still used them.

She sipped on her drink. "That reminds me. I need to pay you for your wonderful services?"

"I don't want anything from you, Mary. How could I possibly charge to find a good friend?"

"You have to eat."

That was true, but he had a pretty good chunk of cash stashed away from his last two cases, and he was getting a retirement from the Navy as well. He didn't answer her, though. Instead, he started looking over the numbers on the fax machine print out. It would take some work tracking down the numbers from the date he suspected the fax would have come in to Caleb's machine. Problem was, he wasn't even sure what he was looking for or if the fax had anything to do with Caleb's departure. Mary could have had more to do with that.

When he realized he would need some help with the numbers, since he couldn't simply call the number and see who answered a fax line, he folded the papers up and shoved them into his back pocket. Mary, who had been propped up against the door frame, raised her glass for a sip and her eyebrows with incertitude.

"Well?" she asked.

"I don't know if the fax means anything," Tony said. "I also have nothing else to go on. Does Kevin know?"

Their son Kevin was a sophomore at the Naval Academy. Tony was Kevin's Godfather. Time had seemed to slip away, and he had not seen Kevin since his high school graduation two years ago. At the time, Caleb was still on active duty, cruising toward retirement, and they were living along Dyes Inlet in East Bremerton.

She shook her head. "No. He's in a pretty structured program. Right in the middle of mid-terms. I didn't want to alarm him."

Before leaving, Tony asked about Caleb's vehicle.

"Last summer Caleb bought a new Ford F250 similar to yours," Mary said. "He really likes the four by four up in the Olympics. His is brown."

"And that's missing, too?"

She nodded her head.

That was interesting. Find a man's truck and the man wouldn't be far away.

CHAPTER 2

The ferry from downtown Seattle to Bremerton took close to an hour on those with cars, thirty-five minutes on a commuter ferry. The car ferry, The Wenatchee, carried up to 2,500 passengers and 218 cars, one of the largest in the Washington State Ferry fleet. Built in 1998, The Wenatchee was also one of the newest ferries. At 460 feet long, and powered by four diesel-electric engines pumping out over 13,000 horsepower, the ferry plowed through the Puget Sound like it owned the waves.

It was windy and cold on the forward observation deck—not many people out there this evening—but shortly after departure from Seattle's Pier 52 at 5:30 p.m., a lone figure dressed in khakis and a Columbia jacket strolled to the bow, his eyes gazing out at Bainbridge Island off the starboard bow in front of him. Now he had to wait. They should have been able to do this somewhere in Seattle. The Pike Brewery or Key Arena. Someplace with more people. He didn't trust this guy or his friends.

Moments later, a stout man of medium height, hair to his shoulders, with two gray streaks along each temple, and a black beard that flowed with the breeze, approached and took a spot along the rail.

The man in the Columbia kept his eyes on the water and said, "We couldn't have done this somewhere else?"

"What better place," the man said, running his hand through his beard. "I was going to Bremerton anyway. I think you know that."

He didn't want to know anything. "I told you I wanted no more contact with you."

"Last time I looked, you didn't have much say in the matter."

A gull floated alongside them before catching a breeze toward the back of the ferry.

The bearded man continued. "Don't be so damn paranoid. You think that gull was bugged? Maybe a tiny camera shoved up its ass?"

"That's not the fuckin' point," Columbia said. He took a second to look back at the glassed-in observation deck behind them. "Look at all those people."

"You insisted on a lot of people. Just keep your head looking at Bainbridge and nobody even knows we're talking." The bearded man hesitated. "Now. . .we still need your help."

What more could he give them? He was tempted to say no, but that could have been a major problem. They knew where he lived. Knew where his kids went to college. They could choose to target them. They could have his ex-wife. But he was stuck and he knew it. "What now?" he asked, defeated.

"We'll let you know," the man said. "I wanted you to know there was more. Just be ready to act when we ask." With that, the man with the beard strolled back inside.

My God, what have I done? He would get to Bremerton and turn right around on the return ferry. Go home and call his kids. Yeah, he was stuck. But maybe he could find a way out.

♦

Back on the stern of The Wenatchee, the man with the beard thought about the cell call he needed to make. What a contrast, he thought. Just last night he wore a two-grand tux, rubbing elbows with Seattle's elite, post-dot.com uber-rich, as they spread their money in support of another liberal cause at a fundraiser to save. . .What the hell was it?. . .some kinda fucking Jumping Frog of Calaveras County. Green Sea Turtle? No, that was last month. It was the Western Snowy Plover. A fine bird, he was sure, but he had been there, like always, for the rare species of clitoris rex. He found them most interesting. And if they ever shut their mouth, liberal women would fuck you to death. Juxtapose last night's grand event with what he was about to do, and he would have to completely change his mindset. That's where his acting training at UW would come in handy.

He made a cell call and waited for an answer. He had that bastard just where he wanted him. Scared shitless and no way out. Now he could manipulate the situation any way he wanted. He smiled to himself, thinking about his comment about the camera up the gull's ass. He'd have to remember to tell the others about that.

A man answered with a "Yeah?"

"It's me. I'm on the ferry." He checked his watch. "Be into Bremerton in a half hour."

"I'll be there."

The bearded man flipped his phone shut and said to himself, "You sure as hell better be." He felt an erection forming in his pants. God, if there was such a beast, would strike him down for what he was thinking. He hesitated, looked up to the sky. Nothing. Just as he suspected. God didn't exist. Or at least he was too busy to worry about his little schemes. He rubbed his firm crotch against the metal railing and smiled. Yeah, he loved when a plan came together.

♦

The brown Ford F250 cruised slowly through downtown Bremerton. Caleb Hatfield had just turned off his cell phone. Sitting in the passenger seat was his friend Pat.

"That him?" Pat asked.

"Arrogant fucker!"

"You knew that going in."

That was true, but he sure as hell didn't have to like it. He downshifted to go up a hill toward the ferry docks.

Caleb said, "I'm not going to park this beast. You go get the bastard." He pulled over to a curb, the ferry landing a couple of blocks away.

"What the hell's the matter with you?" Pat asked. "These people are dangerous. You know that."

Maybe that was the problem. Caleb didn't believe it. Otherwise why would they need the two of them. No, they needed him more than he needed them. He was sure of that much.

"Just go get him, Pat. Everything will work as planned."

Pat looked confused. He wasn't the confident former Army Apache helicopter pilot now. He was just a man who didn't understand everything that was happening. That was Caleb's fault. He was only allowed to tell him so much. And that bothered him. Having both served in the military for so long, they were used to 'need to know' and compartmentalization. But that had always been for national security. Lofty goals indeed.

Reluctantly, his friend left the cab of the pickup, looking back only once on the sidewalk. When Pat had gotten a block down toward the ferry landing, Caleb pulled another phone from under his seat, a secure cell not registered to anyone, and punched in the number from memory.

"Hell of a day?" a man said.

"It gets better," Caleb muttered. He explained how he was about to meet his contact, picking him up at the Bremerton ferry landing. And what they had planned for the night.

When Caleb was done, the man said, "You have to go through with it. Set yourself up as an explosives expert."

Caleb laughed. "What the fuck you think I've been

going for the past twenty-odd years?"

"You know what I meant."

Yeah, Caleb knew. But if he went through with this, he will have crossed the line. His entire past career would have been for nothing. "You sure as fuck better not hang me out to dry."

Release of breath. And then, "Trust me."

"Famous last words. I got nothing. . .shit. They're coming. Gotta go." Caleb quickly hung up, turned off the secure SAT phone, and slid the phone back under the seat.

Look at that arrogant fuck, shuffling down the damn sidewalk like he owns the place. Caleb shook his head. He felt like shoving a stick of dynamite up the man's ass and watching him blow all to hell. This sure as hell better work. Test time, baby.

CHAPTER 3

It was ten minutes to seven in the evening when Tony pulled into the parking lot at the Bremerton American Patriots post. The Patriots, like their counterparts in the American Legion and VFW, was made up of former and active military members from all branches of service. Members, however, were not required to have been in a war. Having all served in the military, Tony suspected most of the members would either be right on time or a little early. He sat in the waning light of spring, his Ford F250 backed into a parking slot, and watched as each person showed up. There was no reason to believe that Caleb Hatfield would come to the meeting, but, since he was the post commander, someone at the meeting might have an idea of where he could have gone. If a bunch of ex-military got together, Tony knew, they'd talk about damn near anything after a couple of beers.

When the crowd entering had dwindled to a trickle, Tony got out and stood alongside his truck. Panzer stood and shook the truck moving from one side to the next.

"Take it easy, Panzer," Tony said calmly. "I'll let you run a little later. You just did your business."

The dog shifted, circled, and settled onto his bed. Tony headed toward the front door. Anyone seeing him enter would probably assume he was either still in the military or recently out. His hair was almost a flat top, and his body was in nearly the best shape of his life as a result of long hikes along the Oregon coast range for most of the late winter and snow-shoeing the Cascades of Central Oregon just prior to that. And, more recently, his hiking with Panzer in the high western Cascades.

The Patriots post for the greater Bremerton area, according to Mary Hatfield, included mostly Navy and Marine Corps veterans who had retired in the area after serving at the Puget Sound Naval Shipyard and the Bangor Submarine Base a few miles north. She also said that the politics of the post were damn near as heated as the Navy itself, with the sub-mariners in constant conflict with the surface sailors. As most sailors knew, there were also turf battles between those who served aboard aircraft carriers and the black shoes, who swayed aboard destroyers, frigates and other surface ships. From the looks of those in attendance this night, there were also many members who were still on active duty from the Middle East wars or the Cold War.

The inside of the building was more impressive than Tony would have guessed, considering the dark-ened state of the outer red brick structure. Here there were photos on the wall dating back to both World

Wars. There were plaques and trophies everywhere. Old uniforms from all of the services, dating back through the years, adorned one full wall. There were also locked cases with the honor guard rifles, which were used for parades and funerals mostly.

Mary had told him he should talk with the assistant post commander, James Webster, a former Navy Captain who had served in Vietnam as a fighter pilot and had spent the last year of that war in the famed Hanoi Hilton in the cell next to Senator John McCain. How would Tony recognize him? He had a full gray beard without the mustache, and he would be conducting the meeting now that Caleb was not there.

Tony saw Webster at the front of the room talking with a younger man, probably a Desert Storm vet, he guessed. A moment later the second in command started the meeting. Tony took a seat in the back row of chairs and listened. The meeting didn't last long. Webster mentioned the Memorial Day parade, the importance of practicing prior to that, and then shifted most into smaller committee meetings. It took the vets a little while to settle into their respective areas, since they first had to grab a fresh beer.

Tony wandered over to a table where Webster sat alone looking over some papers.

"Captain Webster," Tony said, trying his hardest to be both respectful and knowledgeable.

He glanced up from a pair of bifocals. "Have we met?"

Tony reached his hand out to shake. The captain accepted it, shook without great vigor, and nodded for Tony to take a chair across from him.

"No, we haven't met," Tony said. "We have a mutual friend in Caleb Hatfield. We served together for years in Ordnance."

He smiled with that revelation. "You're one of those crazy bastards?" He looked him over carefully. "What? No missing fingers or limbs?"

"No, sir. Just the hearing in my right ear."

"You got a name?"

"Tony Caruso."

The good captain thought for a moment. "You were with the FBI bomb unit in Seattle?"

"Yes, sir. Also worked as an investigator for the ATF on loan for a number of cases."

"Caleb mentioned you," he said. "You want a beer?"

How could Tony refuse that? When the captain returned with two beers, he handed one to Tony and took a long swig from his.

"So, Tony, what can I do ya for?"

Tony hesitated for a microsecond before saying, "I have a matter of discretion I need to discuss with you." As he watched the captain, he knew he shouldn't have started out with such pretension. He sounded more like a lawyer than a friend of Caleb's. Time to get to the point. "I'm trying to find Caleb."

He cocked his head to one side like a confused puppy. "You try his house? You know he moved to Port Orchard."

"Yes, sir. I just came from there, talking with Mary. She gave me your name."

Now Tony's words seemed to be clicking in the

captain's mind. "So, Mary sent you. Fuck me over. She tell you they've been having problems lately?"

"No, sir."

"This is the first meeting Caleb has missed since taking over as commander last September. It's a two year term, and with him retiring last May he said he'd have plenty of time on his hands. Civilian life can be a royal pain in the ass to seagoing sailors. But I guess I'm preaching to the choir."

Tony needed to get him back on track. There was no reason to believe that Captain Webster knew anything about where he could find Caleb, but he might know why he would leave. And that's why Tony was here. "Mary didn't mention any problems."

"Was she drinkin'?"

Suddenly, there was a loud yell from one of the tables, followed by a series of grunting.

"Fuckin' Jarheads," the captain said. "Sometimes I wish they'd join the damn American Legion. That's our best honor guard, though. Where was I?"

"Mary Hatfield?"

"Right. As you probably know, Mary has a tendency to drink a little too much. Has quite the tongue after that." Captain Webster smiled and winked at Tony, as if he should know what he's talking about. Tony did know that she downed damn near half a bottle of Absolut while he was there that afternoon. But she had been quite calm. Depressed even.

"Was her drinking a problem?" Tony asked the captain.

"Let's just say Caleb spent more time here at the club than at home." He hesitated, probably wondering how much to tell a stranger.

"He hang out with anyone in particular here?" Tony asked.

"Mostly me. Some of the other former officers. You get vets together like this and you'd think rank wouldn't matter. But it does. Same guy who used to salute your ass up and down the base now calls you by your first name. But there's always hesitation when they do."

Without saying a word, the captain went back behind the bar and retrieved two more beers. Once he sat down again, he started talking.

"Listen, Tony. How long has Caleb been gone?"

"About a week."

He laughed. "Shit. That barely qualifies for temporary duty. He's probably up in the Olympics catching a creel full of trout. You ever go up there with him?"

Tony admitted he had. Then he asked, "How has he seemed lately?"

Captain Webster shrugged and then narrowed his eyes beneath the bifocals. "I don't know. Now that ya mention it, he was somewhat preoccupied at last week's meeting. He even left early, which is out of character for him. You know what? He was drinking coke like he was in dry-dock."

"That doesn't sound like Caleb," Tony admitted. "Is there anyone else who is usually here but didn't show up tonight? Someone who Caleb might hang out with?"

Captain Webster pulled off his glasses and glanced around the room. "Just the new guy," he finally said. "I call him new, but he's been a member since

November. He's one of the younger guys. Desert Storm. He was an Army chopper pilot flying Apaches, I understand. Blew the shit out of some old Iraqi tanks. Name is Patrick Virtue. He was a warrant officer. He and Caleb hit it off talking about weapons. They also fished together from what I understand. Especially Hood Canal."

"Why's that?"

"Virtue has a place on the canal south of Seabeck. He has a nice boat, fully equipped with navigational equipment, the works."

"You ever go out with them?"

"Hell no. I don't go out on the ocean on anything smaller than a carrier."

Finally, this sounded like a good lead. Tony wondered why Mary hadn't mentioned the guy? "Mary didn't mention him."

"I don't think she ever met the guy," Webster said. "Hell, the wife doesn't need to know everything." He had a sparkle in his eyes.

Since Tony didn't have one, it was hard for him to relate to that. After getting the address for Virtue, he thanked Captain Webster for the info and the beer and headed out.

Sitting in his Ford F250 for a while in the Patriots parking lot, he thought about what Captain Webster had just said. Tony decided it was time to find a place to stay for the night. He could have gone out directly to find Pat Virtue, but he had been to the Seabeck area a number of times, and there was no good way to get there and even a less likely chance of finding the place at night. He knew that task would be hard during the day; damn near impossible in the dark.

Instead, he drove north and found a motel in Silverdale near the mall. He'd head out in the morning for Seabeck.

After he checked in, he pulled out his computer and checked his e-mail. Then he went to his web server, where he had uploaded the files from Caleb Hatfield's computer, and downloaded the temporary internet files from the past three weeks. He could tell immediately that Caleb must have led a pretty boring life. There were a number of photos from porn intro sites, but no actual subscriptions. So someone had probably spammed his e-mail and he had clicked on it out of curiosity. He ignored the cookies, since they rarely gave him anything interesting. Then he checked the actual websites visited. He put them in order of viewing by date. Pretty normal stuff until...bingo!

Three weeks ago Caleb started hitting a number of sites that dealt with the Environmental Defense League, the same organization that had sent Caleb the fax. That gave Tony something to go on. He entered the internet again and started a search of the EDL. Something was familiar about the group, yet there were so many environmental groups in the Pacific Northwest you couldn't drop by a Starbucks without bumping into half a dozen of the faithful.

It didn't take Tony long to jog his memory once he started opening news stories about this group, though. They had caused a shitload of mayhem in Oregon and Washington over the past few years. They were, reportedly, a splinter group from a less radical and respectable group of environmentalists that showed up in force at nearly every major tree cutting and salmon fishery along both coasts. Where the legitimate group had failed to persuade, either by activism or lawsuits, this other group, the EDL, would take the law into its own hands. They were responsible, or had at least claimed responsibility, for nearly every radical act in the past five years. Nobody had died yet, but a few had been injured, including a leading bioengineer from the University of Washington, whose office had been blown to crap with an unsophisticated incendiary device. Now Tony really knew why the EDL sounded familiar, since he had helped with the investigation of that bombing as a member of the ATF task force. He had concluded that a ten-year-old could have set the explosion. Nothing too complex.

The problem with that investigation, and with everything he was reading on the net now, was that nobody had ever been caught from the group. Their bombs and arson jobs might have been unsophisticated, but their planning and dedication to complete secrecy had been nothing less than superb. The FBI had tried and failed to infiltrate the various cells. Problem was, as far as law enforcement was concerned, there was no hierarchy or listing of members or websites or anything that could prove who the members were. Even if the FBI could catch someone doing something, they could keep their mouth shut and none of the other cells would be affected. Maybe not even other members within their own cell. And although many of the attacks were against govern-

CHAPTER 4

W ind whipped across the bow of the 40-foot boat as it cut slowly through the darkness along the western shore of Hood Canal, the long appendage of Puget Sound. Caleb Hatfield felt his long hair flow back in the wind, a feeling unfamiliar to him, as he held tightly to the boat's gunnels. There were no lights on shore, and Caleb knew they couldn't risk turning on their own running lights. But at least the man at the helm could see through his night vision goggles. Keep them from running aground or crashing into dead-heads. Caleb despised douche bags like that bearded freak. Didn't want to deal with him, but knew he had no choice now. He was stuck.

Moments later, the helmsman, Caleb's friend Pat, swiftly turned the wheel and jammed the power into reverse, churning up the water like a bubbling pot to the stern.

"There," the helmsman said. He swung the wheel around, bringing the bow into the waves, and then with precise shifts in power, forward and then backward, the boat responded by drifting closer to shore into a small inlet.

"I can't see shit," Caleb whispered from the bow. He made his way closer to the helmsman. "I don't trust that fucker."

After picking up the man at the Bremerton ferry landing, Caleb and Pat had brought him to Hood Canal, given him a car, and agreed to meet at this remote location with Pat's boat.

"You got the power," Pat whispered back, a little louder than he wanted. Words traveled far across the night water. He lowered his voice. "He gives ya any shit, pop him with your Colt."

With those words, Caleb shoved his elbow against the leather holster under his left arm. "Yeah."

"Come on. Let's do this." Pat made a few final turns of the wheel and then cut the engine.

Caleb hurried to the bow and tried his hardest to see anything along the shore. Any place he could jump to without breaking an ankle. In the darkness he could finally make out the trees along the shore. He grasped the line and was about to jump, when a figure appeared along the shore.

"Throw me a line," the man on the shore whispered loudly.

Without hesitating, Caleb threw the line toward shore. It hit the water with a splash, but the man was able to pick it up, wrap it around a large tree, and start pulling the boat toward shore.

Caleb reached into a side compartment and retrieved a backpack, which he slung over his shoulders, and then settled to the middle of his back and adjusted the straps, the contents rattling about.

"Easy with that," Pat said.

"You drive the boat and let me deal with this."

"Aye, Aye."

"Fuck you!"

The two men moved to the bow. The boat was now lodged against the shore and the stern had swung around with the current and sidled up to the mossy embankment. Caleb and Pat stepped from the boat.

"You guys are right fucking on time," said the man on the bank. The man the two of them knew only as Badger, since his black hair slicked back to beyond his shoulders was streaked on the sides with two three-inch-wide swatches of gray.

Ostensibly, Badger knew them only by code names. That way anyone hearing them talk would not hear their real first names. Caleb was known as Colt, and Pat as Hawk.

Pat pulled off his night vision goggles and considered Badger more carefully. "Where's the car?" he asked.

"Your Bugs a piece a shit! It's up the bank. Pulled into the trees. Looks like folks use it to come down here to fish. You got the stuff?"

Caleb lifted his chin. "Fuckin' right. Let's go do some good."

The three of them made their way through the darkness toward the car. It was a shorter walk than Caleb would have guessed. He would have liked more distance from the road to the canal, just in case the occasional car came along at this hour. Caleb had enough in his backpack for any nosy cop to consider dangerous. Even though most would not even understand what it was until everything came together.

None of them said a word as they got into the VW Bug and drove off to the south, Pat in the front passenger seat, and Caleb, with the heavy backpack, scrunched alone in the back.

A short distance out of Hoodsport, the car slowed and pulled up a dirt road until they wound around a corner out of sight of the main road. The driver shut down the engine.

"We walk from here," Badger said.

"How far?" Pat asked.

"Quarter mile through the woods."

Caleb started to lift his backpack, and then set it back down. "What about the fuel?"

"It's in place. It was put in place last night."

Caleb didn't like this. It could be one big setup. He gets there with his pack, the lights come on, and he's standing there holding his dick. But he didn't have a choice. It was the only way in.

"Let's go," Caleb said, stepping out and hoisting his backpack on with a thud.

"Christ," Badger said, now out and standing next to Caleb. "You tryin' to blow us all to hell?"

"Listen, fuckhead. I don't tell you how to rant and rave, so don't tell me my biz."

Badger's eyes became more intense. "Ease up, dude."

"You girls ready?" Pat quipped. He had placed his night vision goggles on again and his head swiveled around checking the forest for anything unusual. He would now lead them through the woods. There could be no slapping of brushes in faces or cracking of twigs under foot, even though they knew the place would be empty.

At that slow, meticulous pace it took them fifteen minutes to go the quarter mile. Soon they could see a few lights on ahead. Their target.

"Hey," Caleb whispered ahead, stopping the other two. "I thought the place would be empty."

Badger shrugged. "That's the intel I have. The place has looked the same the last five nights."

"Something's wrong," Caleb said.

Badger moved off into the woods a ways and then waved his arms. Caleb and Pat made their way to him and saw the large containers; five plastic six-gallon containers of gasoline.

Caleb immediately removed his backpack and set it in the moist underbrush. Then he clipped a small lamp to his head and clicked it on, illuminating the inside of his bag with a red glow.

"This'll take a couple minutes," Caleb said without looking up at the other two. "Why don't you go ahead and place the gas."

Without saying a word, they each grabbed a gas can in each hand and headed off. Now Caleb watched their dark figures waddling across the open grass area surrounding the log structure. It was too damn light. Something was wrong. He knew it. But it was the only way in. He had to continue. His fingers worked with purpose now attaching the wires. He would wait until he attached them to the cans to set the timers. How much time? Ten to attach the charges to the cans. Fifteen minutes to the car. Another ten to the drop point. Ten or fifteen more to the boat. Shit! He could have made life a lot easier by using a remote signal. He had one that would go a half mile. Next time. They needed to be on the boat and halfway up the canal before they went off. That would give dick-head time to drive off to wherever before all hell broke loose. Better make it forty-five. No need to allow a sprained ankle to fuck up their escape.

A moment later the two men came back, out of breath. Badger was shaking as if it were forty below outside.

"You all right?" Caleb asked the man.

"Yeah. I've done this before, but never with that shit you got there."

"Don't worry. I'll handle all of these; set all the timers. Why don't you haul the last tank so we can get the hell outta here?"

Badger nodded and did as he was told, shuffling off through the grass.

"Hang loose," Caleb said to Pat. "He doesn't look good. Don't let him leave without us." With that, Caleb turned off his light and then headed across the open yard behind the log building. He passed Badger about halfway.

It took Caleb less than ten minutes to move around the perimeter of the building and attach the charges and timer to the gas cans. While he was finishing with the last charge, he stopped for a second when he heard a faint sound. With the wind he wasn't sure of the direction. It could have been behind him in the woods or around the front of the building. And what was that sound? A grunt? A frog. No time. He had to get the hell out of there. With the last charge set and all timers synchronized, he moved across the lawn with purpose.

As he reached the other two, none of them hesitated to say a word. Pat took the lead with his goggles, followed by Badger and Caleb. Moments later they were at the car.

Once inside, Badger started it up and pulled out down the dirt forest service road with only the parking lights showing their way. When they reached the main road, he turned left, flicked on the lights, and sped off.

"Speed limit," Caleb reminded him from the back seat.

"Right, right."

Minutes later they reached the small path that lead down toward the boat. The car stopped just long enough for Caleb and Pat to get out.

Before closing the door, Caleb leaned in and said, "Remember. Speed limit. Get the car back to Hawk's place."

Badger nodded and pulled out onto the road heading north. Caleb checked his watch. The guy should be to Pleasant Harbor by the time it went off. Response would come from the other direction; Hoodsport for fire and Shelton for the sheriff's deputies.

"Let's hustle it up, buddy," Pat said from the trail ahead.

The two of them were back at the boat, shoved off, and cruising north through Hood Canal before they saw a glow off to the southwest. They heard no sirens. Only the waves splashing against the bow. They cruised at a slow, steady pace without lights.

Caleb thought about what he had just done. An act of terror? It was more than a simple protest, a bunch of long-haired tree huggers throwing a wrench in the gears of government. No. This was more than a test. He had a sick feeling in his gut.

CHAPTER 5

Tony startled awake to something on the TV. He shook his head and yawned. On the TV a reporter stood in front of a building surrounded by trees. Although building was now a misnomer, because all that remained of a former log structure was charred lumber. Tony turned up the volume to see what was going on.

A young Chinese reporter, her dark hair cut short, kept glancing over her shoulder. "Investigation into the fire continues. It appears that something, perhaps a propane tank, exploded and started a fire at the Olympic National Forest Station here in Hoodsport. At this time, authorities are still not sure of the cause of the fire. Back to you, John."

The screen flashed to an older news anchor who tried his best to look concerned. "Mai Lu, do we know the identity of the person killed in the blaze?"

Back to the reporter. "We're not sure at this time, John. It was a fluke that they found anyone at all. No one was supposed to be in the building at night. You will remember that the Olympic National Forest has been under some public scrutiny lately, with the controversial issuance of those huge logging permits to Rodgers and Parker Enterprises."

That was all Tony needed to hear. He started to switch channels, when a man passed behind the reporter. It was someone Tony knew from his past in the FBI. Bob McCallum was the senior special agent in charge of the Seattle office. He was Tony's former boss, and probably the biggest reason Tony had joined the private sector after such a short time working with the FBI. What in the hell was Bob doing at a forest service fire?

Something wasn't adding up here. He turned off the TV and light and lay down onto the bed, a streak of light shining in on the wall.

♦

The next morning Tony woke early, let Panzer out of the back of his truck for a run, and then went back into the motel lobby and ate a scant breakfast of coffee and crapy, sticky pastries. After he got back to his room, the rain started falling. Now he watched a nasty rain pound the parking lot pavement from his room window as he drank his third cup of coffee.

As background noise he listened to a local news report on the fire at the Hoodsport forest service station. Investigators had found a male body of indeterminate age but determinate lack of vital signs while rummaging through the burned out hull the night before. There was still no proof that it was anything more than an accidental fire. That was their story, and they were sticking to it.

Tony was pretty damn sure it was more than an accident. Otherwise his good friend, Special Agent Bob McCallum, wouldn't have been anywhere near the joint.

Before he left the motel, he called Mary Hatfield to see if Caleb might have shown up last night. Still no sign of him. He told her to hang in there, and that he'd be out looking into a few leads all day. She wanted him to meet her for dinner at a seafood restaurant in Port Orchard at seven that evening. He agreed and hung up.

He started to leave, but thought for a moment, glancing at the rain pounding the ground. He logged onto his laptop computer and searched for locations of those fax numbers he had gotten from Caleb Hatfield's machine. Some were slam faxes from travel agencies, the kind offering trips to Maui for $300 a week, with the only catch being you have to travel there in a row boat. A few others were local businesses. A law office. A bank. Nothing too interesting. Tony figured those would have a nice new printer, not one of those old dot-matrix contraptions, and no respectable eco-terrorist would work for either of those industries. Nor would they be stupid enough to send a fax about their organization from their own office. Then he saw an interesting pattern, and he should have kicked himself for not seeing it sooner. One number had sent six faxes to Caleb Hatfield over a period of six weeks. He looked up that number and found what he was looking for. It came from one of those anonymous pseudo-mail centers right in

Silverdale; a Mail Outpost. He checked the map and found that it was only two blocks away. Looked like his trip to Seabeck would have to wait a few minutes.

Instead of taking his pickup, he decided to walk to the Mail Outpost. He probably should have known better, considering he had been stationed in the area both on an aircraft carrier and with the FBI, but he decided to take a chance that the rain would clear slightly. Bad idea. By the time he scurried into the Mail Outpost and shook himself off like a drenched duck dog, there wasn't much on his body that his clothes had not stuck to.

There was an older guy behind the counter, glaring at Tony like he was some kind of idiot. Other than that guy, the place was empty.

"Guess I should sell umbrellas," the man said.

Tony ran his fingers through his short hair, thankful he had gotten a military cut a few days back. "I should know better," Tony said. "But sometimes that stuff is deceiving."

Looking at the man more closely, Tony noticed a tattoo of an eagle, an anchor, and two stars on his right biceps. Retired Navy, he guessed.

"What can I do for you?"

"Well, master chief," Tony said. "I need to send a fax."

He limped out from behind the counter and brought Tony to a machine on a table between two copiers.

"It's self serve," he said. "You need some help and you let me know." He started to leave him there, and then stopped and considered him more carefully. "You active duty?" he asked Tony.

"No. Been out for a while. And you?"

He laughed at that. "Christ I coulda served with John Paul Jones." He hobbled back behind the counter.

Tony picked up a piece of white bond paper from a shelf and scribbled a note on it. Then he set it onto the machine and dialed Caleb's number, punched the send button, and waited for it to go through. Glancing back at the chief, Tony noticed the man watching him.

"Everything all right there, partner?" he asked.

"Yeah, thanks."

The paper finished feeding and Tony heard a confirming beep, saying the fax had been sent. He folded the message into his jacket pocket and started toward the counter.

"Sir, could you hit the Report button?"

Tony looked behind him, found the button on the machine, and waited for it to print a session report. Then he read it quickly before handing it to the man.

"You do that after every fax?" Tony asked him.

"Sure do. Gotta keep good records."

"The owner a hard-ass?"

"Yes, but that would be me. I was a yeoman in the Navy and can't quite get over all that cover-your-ass training."

"I see. So you have all these reports filed away somewhere?"

The chief banged his fist against a file cabinet behind him; an upright four-drawer metal unit. Tony imagined he had a file on damn near everything that happened in the place since day one of opening.

"Say I need to find out who sent a fax on a certain date," Tony started, thinking about the list of faxes in his other pocket. "Could you tell me who sent what?"

The old Navy chief scratched his right cheek and then shook his head. "Not likely. I usually don't catch a name unless they pay with a check or a visa. A fax is only a couple of bucks. Most people pay with cash. Why you ask?"

Tony thought about that for a moment. He could try to make him recall a regular who came in faxing with some eco-terrorist letterhead, but the chief would more than certainly tell him to go screw himself. There had to be a better way. Right now that wasn't coming to him, so he paid the guy with cash, thanked him, and was on his way.

Running back to the motel, Tony changed out of his wet clothes and checked out. He rarely stayed in the same motel twice. Not only was that boring, but it went against everything he had been taught in the military on not patterning yourself. He knew that was paranoid. However, it was also like asking him not to take 31-inch strides or fold his underwear—things so ingrained in him that only death or a determined woman could break him of, and neither had come his way yet.

The drive from Silverdale to Seabeck, which under ideal conditions was quite scenic, was a lesson in humility this time. Tony was even forced to put the Ford into four-wheel drive. Once he got to Seabeck, he stopped for a moment to check the address of the former Army helo pilot, Pat Virtue, against a detailed map of Kitsap County. Luckily the rain let up some, enough so that he could actually see about halfway across Hood Canal. Unfortunately, though, the road turned from a winding, paved two-lane, to a winding, dirt almost two-lane. The only consolation was that he would be driving too slow to plow off the edge into the canal or miss Virtue's mail box, assuming he had one.

To say that this part of Kitsap County was a remote area would be like calling Alaska a big state. The houses used to be mostly old cabins from the 40s and 50s, but now the land was worth more than the structures, and many people had built full second homes here on computer software fortunes.

Finally, Tony found the address stenciled not on the actual mailbox, but by surmising from one before and one after that it was the place. The driveway to the house was about a quarter of a mile of bumps and potholes and worn grass. Either Pat Virtue didn't use it much, or he traveled mostly by his boat. Considering the road, it probably was easier to get around in this area, even to buy groceries, by sea.

Tony sat for a moment watching the rain pound his windshield, trying his best to understand what he was looking for in Pat Virtue. Other than the fact that he and Tony's good friend Caleb Hatfield were both missing from a Patriots meeting, and both were fishing buddies, nothing else seemed to tie the two men together. At the very least, though, Caleb could have come to stay with Virtue. That theory was pretty much shot to hell when Tony didn't find Caleb's brown Ford F250 parked on the dirt patch in front of Virtue's house. In fact, there was only an old VW

Beetle tricked out in a Baja package, huge tires full of mud, parked out front.

Glancing down the hill toward Hood Canal, Tony could see the dock through flowing wisps of fog, but there was no boat moored to the side.

The rain gave up a bit, so he got out and went to the front porch. The house was like a refuge the old timers used to plop down to escape an ever-increasing urban society in the 40s, or perhaps a Depression-era shack used to avoid the tax collector. Either way, it looked like Virtue had plans for the future. There was a new wooden structure, a rain deflector mostly, with stacks of lumber covered further by large blue tarps. Yeah, he was going to build something, or maybe tear down the current structure and start over from scratch on a new place.

Out of courtesy Tony knocked on the door, not really expecting an answer. Nothing. He peered through the door, but didn't see anything to indicate Caleb was there or had been there. He was beginning to think his drive out had been nothing more than an exercise for his windshield wipers. But he decided to look a little more closely. He walked around the side of the house, glancing into windows as he went. The windows were plastered with rain, making it almost impossible to see inside. And he felt a little strange peeping into windows. He half expected to see the barrel of a shotgun poking out at his nose. Instead of continuing, he walked down toward the dock. There were a few recent tracks in the mud where someone with big feet had roamed. It looked like the same person had made all the marks. Walking out on the dock,

Tony didn't find anything out of the ordinary. This was a waste of time, and the rain was starting to come more heavily again. He hurried back to his truck and scurried behind the wheel.

Before leaving, he thought of something. He got out again and let Panzer out of the back. The large black dog ran immediately toward the VW Beetle, sniffing around and concentrating on the passenger door. Then just as Tony thought the dog would stay there, it burst off toward the house, ran around the back, and eventually showed up out front again, hanging around the front door. Something had Panzer excited. But that was the problem with having a dog that had been trained initially to detect explosives. Once the training ceased, that wonderful nose would pick up on anything from old friends to jelly dough-nuts. There was no concrete distinguishing sign that the dog would give him to allow Tony to understand the hit.

Now Tony was stuck. He had run out of ideas. He whistled for Panzer, who ran full speed and jumped into the back of the truck. Tony gave him a scratch along the ears and the dog responded by licking his hand. He closed the dog into the topper and got back behind the wheel.

Since the rain was going to make his day miserable anyway, he decided to take a little drive to Hoodsport.

Seeming to remember that the only way to cross or get around Hood Canal was by going over the Hood Canal bridge to the north or skirting around it on the south and west, he decided on the later. By water the trip would take a lot less time, but by car the trip would be perhaps an hour with this weather. As it was, the drive took him forty-five minutes. The rain had given way to swirling clouds to the south.

When he finally pulled up to the parking lot to what had been the Olympic National Forest office, Tony noticed two things. First, the building now resembled the aftermath of a college bonfire. And second, there was yellow boundary tape telling everyone to stay the hell away.

Tony got out of his truck and gazed upon the scene. Panzer. He let his dog out but put him on a short leash. Then he stepped up to the tape, Panzer at his right side. Looking around behind him, he shrugged and stepped under the tape. Immediately he was transformed back to his FBI and ATF days, sifting through rubble and ash for clues. It was a nasty job. One which he no longer had the stomach for either. Part of him wondered why there were no cops or feds hanging around the joint. After all, since they did find a body, this was a crime scene. That is unless they determined it was an unfortunate accident.

Panzer strained against the leather leash, so Tony let the dog claw his way toward the outer shell of the building. The dog's nose was now on a spot of charred grass.

Tony gave the signal to search more and the dog turned around and led him across the grass of the back yard toward the forest. A few yards into the wet forest, Panzer stopped again, his nose moving back and forth. Pulling on the leash, Tony led the dog back toward the former forest service headquarters.

Just in front of him, toward the back of the building, there was an area cordoned off where they had
probably found the body. They had probably brought
the man to the lab in Olympia, Tony guessed.

Suddenly, he heard a car rolling into the driveway.
He turned to see a newer Ford Taurus, dark as the
ash, stop next to his Ford F250. A man dressed in a
wrinkled suit got out from behind the wheel, and a
woman who looked far more fresh slid out from the
passenger side.

Damn!

"What the fuck are you doing in my crime scene?"
the man yelled. He had his right hand on his hip rested against his 9mm Beretta.

How did Tony know it was a Beretta? Because the
man behind the gun was FBI Special Agent Bob
McCallum. He didn't know the woman, but he
guessed, considering her looks, she was the newest
agent trying to beat off the advances of McCallum.

Tony started toward the boundary tape. "You got
one hell of a horseshit memory, Bob."

Special Agent McCallum considered Tony more
carefully now. Then he shook his head. "Caruso,
what in the fuck are you doin' here? I thought you
were down in Bumfuck, Oregon."

The woman gazed at her boss. "You know this
guy?"

"Carrie, just shoot him," McCallum said. "It'll be
much less paperwork in the long run. Go ahead!"

Tony crossed the tape and stepped into the wet
grass, wiping his shoes off the best he could. Panzer
took a seat on the grass at his side. The woman,

Carrie, was trying to figure out if her boss was kidding.

"Bob, you still got a fucked up attitude," Tony reminded him.

McCallum turned to his partner. "This piece a shit used to work for me. Until I sent him packing into the private sector."

"I quit! And I was only a consultant."

"Yeah, and I got a ten-inch dick."

Tony laughed. "Remember, we used to play basketball together. The showers?"

"Fuck you!"

"Not with that puny dick of yours."

"Boys, boys," the woman said. "Can you cut with the macho bullshit?"

Feeling compelled to let their past slide, Tony extended his hand to shake. Reluctantly, Bob McCallum accepted and didn't even try to squeeze the life out of his hand.

"There," Carrie said. She reached out her hand to Tony, and after they shook, she said, "Carrie Jones."

"Tony Caruso."

"Like the tenor?" she asked.

"Are you a friend of opera?"

She nodded. "Every chance I get."

"And yes, my family is actually related to the great Enrico Caruso."

Her eyes brightened. "Really?"

"All right, all right, shut the fuck up the both of you." McCallum stuck his finger into Tony's chest. "What in the fuck you doin' here, asshole? Lettin' that damn dog of yours run free in my area. Shitin' and pissin' on my crime scene."

Tony simply stared at him and shook his head. When his old boss failed to budge, he turned to Carrie and said, "Would you tell your boss to get laid once in a while? And beatin' off in the shower doesn't count."

McCallum took a step toward Tony, and then stopped. He might have been thinking about the last time they got in a physical altercation. Tony's old boss had had to deflect questions about the black and puffed up eye for more than a week. At the time he should have known better, since he had read Tony's personnel file, which mentioned his martial arts training. Yet, some guys seem to think that all that fancy kicking and stuff is for those who are physically inferior, and brut strength alone is all that mattered. McCallum was one of those. He was in good shape, though. He worked out on weights at least three times a week, and wore tight shirts to prove it to the world. But, Tony had put the guy off long enough. After all, the guy did have Tony by the balls. Tony had crossed the yellow police tape. Rules were rules for McCallum. He stood there waiting for Tony to answer.

"All right," Tony started. "I was sitting in my motel room last night in Silverdale and saw you on the news. I just had to see you, Bob."

"Cut the shit," McCallum said. Then he turned to his partner. "This fucker couldn't tell the truth if his life depended on it."

She was smiling, but said nothing.

McCallum continued, "You don't go anywhere

unless someone's paying you, Caruso."

Ouch. That hurt. "Really. I did see you on the news last night, scrounging around behind that cute Chinese reporter."

"Did you see her?" McCallum said. "She's a little hottie."

"Boys. Can you put your instruments of pleasure away for a couple minutes?"

"Right, sorry," Tony said. "So what do you have on the crispy critter?"

"We..." McCallum started. "Hey, none of your fuckin' business."

"They said it was an accident," Tony said. "But now we all know that's a bunch of shit or the local sheriff would be investigating this."

"This is federal property," Carrie reminded Tony.

She had him there, and he should have thought of that. "True. But you could have sent someone from the Olympia office. Or even some underling from your Seattle office. But why send the special agent in charge of this area? Bob, you weren't demoted were you?"

"Bite me!"

Now Tony had the both of them and they knew it.

McCallum seemed to sense this, so he quickly said, "What I decide to investigate is none of your business. You still haven't told me why you're here."

Damn. He thought he had deflected that question. Finally, Tony briefly explained how he was looking for his good friend, Caleb Hatfield. McCallum had actually met Caleb a few times. Tony left out some important details. Things that might even explain why he was really there. If only Tony knew that himself.

"It still doesn't explain why you would come here looking for Caleb Hatfield," McCallum said.

He had a point. Tony wished he could answer, but even he wasn't sure about that. He had a strange feeling that this fire involved the group that had faxed Caleb. How that mattered was another point all together. Time to go fishing.

"You ever hear of the Environmental Defense League?"

When McCallum's brows rose and his partner cocked her head to one side, Tony knew he had his answer.

McCallum spoke first. "You know we have, Caruso. Damn, you and I worked on that horse corral fire down in Oregon together."

Carrie nodded in agreement. "That was before my time. I think I was in college, but I heard about it."

"You two are the worst fuckin' actors on the west coast," Tony said. "Christ almighty, take some lessons."

There was silence for a long minute.

Finally, McCallum couldn't take it any longer. "You know something about this group?"

"Maybe. You know something about human decency?"

Carrie laughed. Tony had an audience of one.

McCallum shook his head and said, "All right. Enough with the feeling out. What do you know about the EDL?"

"I'm guessing we're standing in front of their latest

work," Tony said, nodding toward the burnt building.

McCallum tried not to glance over his shoulder, but Tony saw his neck strain in that direction. "We don't know what happened here, yet."

"But you have your suspicions."

Carrie glanced at her boss. She looked like she wanted to say something, but wasn't sure how much she could tell Tony.

When McCallum failed to speak, Tony continued, "You got a fax didn't ya? With the EDL claiming responsibility."

"How the..." McCallum stopped himself. "It doesn't mean shit. We also got a call from some other wacho saying he didn't do it."

"Let me guess. That call came after it was reported that a body was found inside."

The two of them looked at each other, and then McCallum said to me, "What's your point?"

"The point is, the EDL has never killed someone before. It fucks their cause all to hell if they're labeled murderers. They want the people behind them. They want the people to see them as noble crusaders against the tyranny of the establishment and the greedy lumber companies who have raped this land for profits and built huge houses for the rich."

"You sound like you could be a member," McCallum said, not even a hint of smile on his face.

"We are all members," Tony said. "Why do you think you have found nothing on this group in the past ten years?"

Now Carrie was interested enough to shift her gaze sideways at her boss. She too wanted an answer.

"You know why, smartass," McCallum said. "Why don't you enlighten us?"

"Because...because they have no roster. They have no website. They have no leader. They have no head-quarters. They are a group within no other group. They have cells that are not attached. You catch one, which you have never done by the way, and that one leads to no other person. That, my friend, is why they are such a thorn in your ass. You can't catch what you can't find. And all of this, or at least most of it, is happening in your back yard. That just drives you fucking crazy. Not to mention your boss in Washington. They gotta be going nuts about now. Threatening to send your ass to Duluth, McCallum?"

McCallum had listened carefully, not saying a word. Finally, he shook his head and said, "Fargo."

"Shit. I'm sorry, man." When neither of them said anything, Tony continued, "You do think the EDL was involved here, though."

"Yeah—"

"Carrie, shut the fuck up!"

"He could help us," she said.

McCallum thought about it. Apparently he agreed. "Something isn't right about this, though. You are right. They faxed us responsibility. Then someone called later this morning saying the fax had been sent in error. We traced the call to a phone booth in Bremerton."

"And the fax came from a Mail Outpost in Silverdale," Tony said, guessing.

"How the fuck did you know that?" McCallum yelled.

"Lucky guess. Continue."

"That's all we've got," he said.

"You said something doesn't fit with this bombing," Tony reminded him.

"He's got ya there, sir," Carrie said.

"The fire in the past, as you know, were the result of unsophisticated incendiary devices that any fuck could learn to do from watching T.V. These, though, show a progression of knowledge."

"Could have gotten that on the internet," Tony said.

"Maybe. But I don't think so."

"Why not?"

"They're using military technology and techniques."

That's not what Tony wanted to hear. The farthest thing from it, in fact. Now he felt like a shithead, having mentioned Caleb Hatfield. McCallum knew exactly what Caleb had done in the Navy for more than twenty years.

The only other thing Tony found out from those two was that the dead man found in the remains of the ash was one of the nineteen employees who worked at the forest service office. He and his wife had been having problems, so he was camping out there on a cot. Nobody knew he was there, and it was only a fluke that he was. Tony put Panzer in the back and drove off.

CHAPTER 6

By the time Tony got back from Hoodsport, it was closing in on 7 p.m. He was supposed to meet Caleb's wife Mary for dinner at the Sinclair Seaside Restaurant, a nice place on the pier next to the marina. He parked alongside a public park a couple blocks away and walked slowly toward the restaurant. The rain that had fallen earlier in the day had given way to swirling clouds and a hint of a sunset. It was the kind of evening that had scared the shit out of him as a sailor, because a huge storm usually followed.

Checking his watch before entering the restaurant, he realized he was right on time. Damn military had done that to him.

He found Mary Hatfield at a window table staring off across the bay toward the Bremerton shipyard. She had one hand wrapped in a death grip around a short glass of clear liquid and ice, probably vodka again, while her other hand rested on the wooden windowsill.

Tony sat down across from her and she finally

noticed he had arrived. She was wearing blue jeans, tennis shoes, and a puffy red sweater that matched her eyes.

"Been here long," Tony asked.

She raised her glass. "This is my first glass, if that tells you anything."

Actually, it did. She must have just sat down. When she didn't say anything, Tony asked, "Any word from Caleb?"

She shook her head and then took a long gulp of vodka.

"You get my fax?" Tony asked her.

She reached into her purse and retrieved a piece of white paper folder in half. She handed it to Tony.

He looked over the paper carefully but he couldn't tell anything from that. Although a fax might not be any old fax, what he really needed was the printer that had been used first.

"Is it the same as the last one?" she asked.

"I don't know. I can't tell. Doesn't really matter. I need the source printer."

The waiter came through and Tony ordered a local microbrew. Mary asked for another vodka on the rocks. Neither of them said a word until the drinks arrived, an excruciating couple of minutes. Tony wasn't sure what to tell Mary. As far as he knew, Caleb could have driven his truck east to visit one of his old navy buddies. Caleb had a brother in Kentucky and a sister in Iowa, but Mary had said she had already called each of them with no luck. They assured her that Caleb would show up eventually. He's a responsible guy. Everybody knew that. Yeah,

Tony also knew that, and that's what was so disturb-
ing.

"What's going on, Mary?"

She whipped around. "What?"

"I can smell the guilt on you. It's seeping from your
pores."

"Are you sure that's not the vodka?" She tried a
smile but it came across her face crooked, like someone had smacked her right in the middle of the
attempt.

"Listen. If you want me to continue looking for
Caleb, just say the word. But in doing so, you sure as
hell better tell me every God damn thing you know."

Her hand that cradled the vodka glass started shaking, rattling the ice against the side, until she grasped
the glass with her other hand.

"Well?" Tony relented.

She let out a heavy sigh and said, "I don't know
what to say. You think you know someone." She hesitated, her eyes piercing through him, trying their
best to ask for forgiveness or understanding or something.

"I'm sorry," he said. "It's just that you haven't
given me much to go on."

Finally, she said, "We've been having problems."
With that revelation she seemed to settle down some.
Either the vodka was working, or she felt good about
telling him something she probably had failed to
realize herself.

"And?"

"And...there's not much to tell. Caleb retires and
goes fishing. Our son goes off to the Naval Academy.

The ladies down at the officer's club start giving me the cold shoulder because we are no longer active duty. The tennis dates get farther and farther apart. I just didn't think this is how it would be. I thought retirement would somehow be...more exciting."

"You should have plenty of time with Caleb. You could travel together, play tennis, whatever."

She shook her head. "The Navy was everything to Caleb. You know that. He retires and starts pacing back and forth in the house like a caged lion. I told him to get the hell out."

Now Tony was confused. "You told him to leave?"

"No. No. Not like that. I told him to find a hobby. Find a passion." She stopped to take a drink.

"Did he?"

"He joined the Patriots," she said. "Then last November he started fishing again. He was always gone doing that. I told him to find a damn passion, and he really jumped in with both feet." The resentment in her voice was obvious. Caleb had found some solace where she had not.

Tony needed to get her back on track. "But you said you were having problems. The fishing didn't work for him?"

"Oh, it worked for him. It just didn't work for us. I thought we could at least do something together. But he was always up in the mountains or out in the sound." She glanced out the window at the water as if looking for her husband.

Tony knew retirement from any military service was difficult. It had not been easy for him, yet it was probably not as rough since he only had himself to piss off. He had heard that a fairly high percentage of retired military ended their own life or simply drank themselves to death because of the lack of purpose they found in civilian life. Spouses must have fit into the equation similarly.

"You know a guy named Pat Virtue?" Tony asked her.

She peered at him carefully, uncertain. "I think he's called the house a few times. Someone from the Patriots, maybe."

"You've never met him, then?"

She swished her head and her drink flowed back and forth until she brought it to her mouth and finished it off. Then she raised her glass to the young waiter, who was off for round three.

Once she got her drink, she said, "You think he might be with this guy?"

"I don't know. Maybe. I went out to the guy's place today, but he wasn't home. I had heard from Captain Webster that Caleb and Virtue had been hanging out together fishing. Virtue owns a boat. But the boat wasn't hitched to the dock, and Caleb's truck wasn't around."

"Maybe Caleb parked in town and the guy picked him up somewhere with the boat."

Tony had already thought of that. But he had not found Caleb's truck in Seabeck either. And with a town that small, it was likely a strange truck would stand out like a pimple on a homecoming queen.

"I haven't given up yet, Mary," he said. "I just need more to go on. Anything you could tell me would help."

She thought hard, her forehead wrinkling. "I've thought of everything."

"You said you were having problems," he reminded her. "What kind of problems?"

Reluctantly, she said, "He didn't want me anymore."

"You were thinking of divorce?"

"I don't know. He just didn't want me."

"Physically?"

"Yes! We had sex once a month," she yelled, and when she noticed people staring at her, she turned her head out to sea, her face as red as her eyes.

After that the evening got even more strange. Tony had come there thinking he would eat something, since he hadn't eaten a thing after the continental fare from the motel, but Mary didn't seem in any hurry to eat. Besides, she had her ice to chew on and her vodka to chase that down. Instead he ordered a basket of fries and nibbled while Mary talked about all the sex she wasn't having. He realized he wasn't going to get anything more out of her. She just wanted to rant at someone. Tony would be the first to admit that he wasn't a perfect listener, but every now and then he surprised himself. While she was off in the bathroom peeing or puking or whatever it was women do in there, he got a call on his cell phone. That was strange enough in itself, because not many people had his number. And he sure as hell hadn't given it to Pat Virtue.

"How'd you get this number?" Tony asked him.

"Never mind! I heard you were out at my place lookin' for me. What do you want?"

He had an interesting accent, but Tony was having a hard time placing it. It was somewhere between country redneck and southern backwater. "Missouri Ozark," Tony said.

"What?"

"Never mind."

After a moment, Virtue said, "I asked you a question, Dickhead."

Tony hung up on him. He never put up with obnoxious people, especially on his dime and his time.

The phone rang again just as Mary sat down across from him. She actually looked better. He guessed she had gone through a thorough hurling cleanse.

"You gonna answer that?" she asked, pointing at the phone in his hand.

He waited for the sixth ring and then answered, "Listen. Don't waste my time. You know damn well why I was out at your place, otherwise you wouldn't have this number. Now why don't you cut the bullshit and tell me what I need to know?"

Pat Virtue, who had been so silent on the other end Tony thought he had actually hung up, finally let out a heavy breath. "I've heard you can be a pain in the ass. Just stay the hell out of this. You're in too deep already."

Tony sat looking at his phone somewhat dumbfounded. He didn't know this Pat Virtue any better than the guy who had been bringing him beer for the past hour. Even less. At least he knew what the waiter looked like. Now he had been warned to stay out of this. What the hell was this? Find Caleb. That's all he was trying to do. Meanwhile, Mary was sitting across from him trying to read his face. Yet, this message had not really come from Pat Virtue. He was the one who spoke the words. But the words were from Caleb Hatfield. Tony was certain of that.

♦

Tony gave Mary a ride home and told her she could come back for her car in the morning. She had asked a few questions about his strange call, but he had deflected those with cryptic words like business and nobody and it's nothing. He sure as hell didn't want to let her know what he suspected...that her husband Caleb was probably within a few miles of their little liquid dinner. At least that's what he guessed and hoped to be true.

After dropping her off, he drove southwest for a ways on a country road until he found a little dirt track that angled back into the woods. He drove down the road a short distance until he found a spot where the Ford pickup would fit among the grass and pines. The beauty of traveling everywhere with his bed over his shoulder, was that he could just about sleep anywhere a cop wouldn't knock on the window to see if he was still alive. Most of the time he found places that most would never even consider as a place to stay the night.

He and Panzer both took a long leak before climbing into the back of the truck for the evening.

In the back of his full-bed pickup he had an air mattress that filled up most of the space. His dog, Panzer, had a small pad at his feet. Tony's clothes hung along one side and in containers, and the windows of the topper were tinted to keep out the light and prying eyes. He could slide windows on both sides to allow a cross breeze, and the screens kept out unwanted bugs. It was comfortable back there for a couple of nights, but then he needed a place to wash up. For the last six months, he had been staying first at a friend's condo in Bend, Oregon, and ended up solving what was thought to be a murder suicide. The last couple of months he had been back to his home state of Minnesota, and then back to the Oregon coast. With that quick case in Idaho sandwiched between.

Since leaving the military, he had never gotten around to finding a permanent home. He had started working as a consultant for the FBI bomb unit in Seattle, on loan to damn near every law enforcement unit in Washington, Oregon, Idaho and Montana, with a few jaunts into Alaska. There was no need to buy a house under those circumstances, and even less once he was assigned to the ATF, traveling to anything that blew up across the country. Now, although he could have settled into one location and actually plopped down money on a house, he just wasn't sure where he wanted to call home.

So he lay in the back of his converted Ford truck, the windows open a crack letting in the night air, and wondered what in the hell Pat Virtue had meant with his words. Or Caleb's words. Somehow, Caleb wanted him to back off. But back off of what? The crickets and frogs were talking loud and clear, but they sure weren't giving him a clue. Even Panzer was snoring now.

CHAPTER 7

Caleb didn't like this one bit. He and Pat were driving slowly up the forest service road toward The Brothers Wilderness, the night as dark as the inside of his churning gut, and the tires of his 4x4 truck slipping and sliding like a two-year-old on an ice rink.

"This is bullshit," Caleb said to Pat. "We take all the risk on this one, while that skunk-headed dink hangs out in the woods."

The truck hit a bump in the road and the containers in the back landed with a thump. They had strapped them down with bungee cords, but there was always a little give. No getting around that.

"Easy," Pat said. "You tryin' to kill us?"

"The thought had crossed my mind."

"What the fuck is wrong with you?" Pat said, pulling a cigarette from his front pocket and shoving it into his mouth. "You've been sulking for two days."

"Don't even think of lighting up," Caleb said.

"Yeah, right." Pat shifted his eyes over his shoulder

to the truck bed and then put the cigarette back in its pack. "Well? What's goin' on?"

Caleb let out a deep breath. "Those fuckers are gonna hang us out to dry."

"Skunk Head? I'll kick his ass."

"No. The others."

"Hey. We had no idea some dumbass forester was callin' that place home. Shitforbrains. Some guys are just in the wrong place at the wrong time."

That's the way Caleb felt tonight. The other night as well, burning the shit out of a perfectly good building. He had no idea how that would help their cause. They'd end up cutting down more trees to rebuild the forest service headquarters. And they'd probably build a bigger structure than the one they had destroyed. That was brilliant. Insurance rates go up for the government and more trees hit the dirt. Tonight made a little more sense. But, he knew, or at least suspected, there was more to all of this. More than he or Pat were being told. That's what had his gut in a knot.

He pulled the truck up a final grade and their target became more clear. To the left side of the road the trees had been cut and a clearing made. Caleb turned left onto a makeshift drive that led to the clear-cut, and the headlights shone on the massive logging equipment.

Suddenly, the man with the skunk-hair, Badger, stepped out from behind a skidder, his hands in the air.

Caleb shut down the truck, cut the lights, and sat for a moment, the night breeze seeping through both cab windows.

Badger came up to the driver's window. "Right on fuckin' time again. I like workin' with you guys."

"Where's your car?" Pat asked him.

His upper lip rose and a sneer crossed his mouth. "Road a mountain bike I acquired in Seabeck. I'll need a ride back down the hill."

Caleb opened the door, almost hitting the man in his chest, and then stepped down from the cab. "Let's get this over with. I don't like the idea of one way in and one way out. All we need is some pilot spotting the fire and calling it in. They set up a road block and we're fucked."

Badger followed Caleb to the back of the truck, and Pat met them there from the other side.

"Loosen those tie-downs," Caleb ordered. He had stopped asking and started demanding. The contents of the bed were covered with a large green tarp. He had no intention of letting anyone see what he had there. Pulling a mini-mag from his pocket, Caleb shone the light on the contents of the bed.

"This'll be enough?" Badger asked. He bit his lip now with excitement, like a kid in a spelling bee.

Caleb laughed. "Yeah. There's enough shit here to burn a city block back to basic elements."

"Cool," Badger said, and then clicked his tongue a couple times inside his mouth.

Shaking his head, Caleb started pulling the materials toward the back of the truck bed. Pat helped by jumping into the back and pushing. The plan was rather simple, but the execution was much more complex. They would coat the logging equipment with the compound and then Caleb would set it off with a remote control.

They were in place with the materials next to the first target, a large logging truck.

"Start pumping that," Caleb said to Badger.

"I don't understand why we couldn't use a generator compressor," Badger complained.

Caleb shook his head as he grabbed the hose and nozzle. "Well, we could have. But there's always the possibility of a spark igniting this shit. This crap would blow all of us halfway to Seattle."

The man started pumping now. "Gotcha. By the way, what is this shit?"

Caleb looked back at Pat, who was still positioning containers alongside the logging equipment. "It's kind of like Napalm. A fuel gel mix. The consistency has to be thick enough to stick to the metal, but thin enough to spray on." Just as he finished explaining the compound, Caleb pulled the trigger on the spray nozzle and the fuel/gel mixture flew out onto the side of the truck. It didn't take him long to cover the entire truck cab. Then they moved on to the bed, with the long tines that held the logs in place.

By now Pat had all of the containers set up next to the equipment, waiting to be attached to the sprayer. There were five major pieces of equipment, including a front loader, skidder, and the truck. When Caleb was almost done with the last truck, he handed the nozzle over to Pat to finish the job.

"I gotta get the detonators set," Caleb said, turning toward his truck.

"Why don't we just light a match?" Badger asked.

Caleb stopped and turned. "You really wanna get close enough to drop a match? Listen, asshole, you let me deal with the pyrotechnics. You handle the PR." He walked back to the truck.

When Caleb was gone, Badger asked Pat, "What's his problem? He's tighter than a duck's ass."

Not missing a stroke, Pat said, "He's serious about this shit. He's a professional, though. So, don't question him on this stuff. The guy's a genius at blowin' shit up."

Badger glanced toward the truck at Caleb. "Intense."

The two men finished off the last of the fuel/gel and then hauled the pump, hose and nozzle onto the bed of the last truck they had sprayed. No sense saving any of it. It was all they needed to get caught driving down the mountain with remnants of the fuel/gel mixture. There would be no way to explain that.

♦

It took Caleb another ten minutes to place the small charges on each piece of logging equipment. He was using a simple igniter attached to a battery pack that would be detonated from nearly a mile away. In fact, on a clear night, which this was not, he knew the signal would go for miles. But, with the terrain and the trees he wanted to make sure the signal was strong, so they would drive down the mountain about a mile and hit the button.

Before taking off, Badger set his mountain bike

into the back of Caleb's truck and strapped it in. Then they covered the bed with the tarp again and climbed inside.

Caleb sat for a moment, thinking, making sure everything was set properly. He was back in his training now, his eyes closed, running the sequence through his mind down to the most insignificant detail. 'The details were what would get you killed,' he remembered his friend Tony always said. Convinced that everything was right, he started the truck and put it in gear, the tires spinning some and blending in with the rest of the tracks in the clearing.

A few minutes later, down the road a ways, Caleb pulled the truck to the side of the road, almost getting stuck in the mire. He took out the small transmitter and hesitated.

The three of them turned to look out the cab window.

Caleb smiled and then pressed the button.

Nothing.

"Fuck," Badger yelled.

"Hang on," Pat said.

Caleb aimed the transmitter again and pressed the button.

Still nothing.

"Shit," Caleb said, putting the truck into gear and pulling out onto the muddy road sideways.

Just for the hell of it, he tried the transmitter again. There was a flash up the road, followed by a huge ball of flames that burst as high as the trees.

They all let out a yell of approval.

"Fuckin' right," Badger screamed, his eyes mesmerized by the glow in the distance. "I wish we were there, closer, so we could see the flames."

But by now Caleb had the truck straightened out and they were hauling ass down the road. From time to time, Caleb would glance back at the glow in his rearview mirror.

He thought about his past. How in the hell had it come to this? Sure it had been his job to make things go boom when they were supposed to, but that had always been far away from the carrier at some unseen target. He had always wondered what the pilots were thinking when they pickled their bomb buttons. He thought back on his trip with Tony Caruso to the jungles of Java, seeing the damage those bombs could do up close. The two of them would have to live with that sanitation job for the rest of their lives—a bond that neither of them really wanted to remember.

CHAPTER 8

Tony got up Saturday morning thinking it was still night. It was so dark it was hard to tell. He had gotten out to take a leak and allowed Panzer to do the same, when his prediction about the strange clouds from the night before had come true. One wicked storm burst upon them just as Tony had gotten Panzer into the back and him into the driver's seat. The biggest problem was the wind, Tony thought. He could feel the truck shaking back and forth with each gust.

Damn! He had wanted to take a run or brisk hike after being confined to the truck bed. Now he was stuck. He started heading back toward town. He got almost all of the way down the road when he braked hard. Spread out across the muddy road was a pine tree six inches in diameter, knocked over by the ugly winds. Now, most people would have gotten out and tried to budge the thing out of the way. Tony simply popped the truck into four-wheel-drive and ambled over the tree.

The darkness made him believe his watch had

stopped, but the radio confirmed the time and the local DJ also said that a number of roads in the area were closed because of fallen trees and power lines. So he drove into Port Orchard for a java jolt at a little cafe, along with a nice round of cholesterol in the form of a three-egg omelet and butter-slathered hash browns. He had a feeling the day would be long, and he wanted something in his body that would stick with him for most of the day.

He ate at the counter, with an older waitress filling his coffee cup with each pass. It was still early and there were only a couple of old timers, most likely local regulars, sitting at a table. The radio played country western until a man came on with a breaking story. The waitress stopped, turned up the volume, and listened carefully.

There had been another incident. That's what they called it. An incident. This time a number of logging trucks and skidders had been torched near The Brothers Wilderness Area. The announcer wanted to remind the listeners that the equipment was owned by Rodgers and Parker Enterprises, the logging company that was currently cutting on the edge of the Olympic National Park on a permit issued by the Olympic National Forest.

"Crazy bastards," the waitress said, shaking her head. She turned her gaze on Tony. "You know who makes out in a deal like this? The lawyers. 'Course they make out on every deal. But it always comes down to the lawyers."

"You know about this logging company?" Tony asked her.

Before she answered, he noticed the two old timers taking an interest in their conversation.

She poured more coffee in his cup and said, "Sure. They come in here all the time. A bunch live right here in town."

One of the older guys spoke up now. "Did they say those enviro-whackos just torched some perfectly good equipment?"

"Sure did," the waitress said.

"Actually, they didn't say who did it," Tony reminded all of them.

"Bullshit!" the old guy said. "Everybody knows those cappo-chino drinkin' tree-huggin' hairy-legged turds did it. They all got shit for brains if you ask me."

"Nobody asked, Walt," the waitress said. "Besides, how do we know this young fellow here isn't one of them."

"Come on, Doris, look at him," the guy said. "Sure he needs a shave. But he's wearin' nice slacks and a London Fog coat. Damn near got a high and tight haircut like a jarhead. If he ain't prior military, then my breakfast should be free."

Actually, the coat was a Helley Hansen, but Tony thought he should throw the dog a bone, since such great insight should always be rewarded. Besides, they might know something about something. He swiveled in his chair toward the two men.

"You got me, gents," Tony said. "Former Navy Ordnance."

They both raised their eyes with that. To impress a former sailor, just mention you were either Ordnance or a SEAL.

"You crazy bastard," Walt said. He looked Tony up and down. "Still got all your limbs and major organs. You must have been a good one."

The waitress looked confused. "I don't get ya."

"Ordnance, Doris. Crazy bomb jock. Used to work on the flight deck of carriers. These are the guys you see on T.V. who load bombs and missiles and nukes on aircraft on a pitching deck out in the damn ocean." He shook his head and mumbled something under his breath.

"Are you two retired Navy?" Tony asked.

"Yeah, we spent some time scrapin' barnacles from those gray devils." He shifted his head toward the ships across the bay.

Tony smiled with that. "You know a guy in town named Caleb Hatfield? Just retired as a commander."

The two thought for a moment, not coming up with anything. But Tony got a hit with Doris the waitress.

"I know Caleb Hatfield," she said. "He comes in here sometimes and eats those omelets like you. Lives just up the hill a ways."

"That the guy with the brown leather bomber jacket?" Walt asked.

"Yeah, that's him."

"I know him," Walt said. "A nice fellow for an officer."

"We served together," Tony said.

"He's Ordnance?" the guy asked.

"Was until he retired a short while ago."

"I haven't seen Caleb in a while," Doris said. "He's been coming in to fill up his thermos before going off fishing. He usually comes in here Saturday mornings. That's today. Hmm...he's pretty religious about that."

That's a fact Tony also knew. Something his wife Mary had told him. "I've been trying to find him for a couple of days," Tony admitted. "He promised me a couple of good beers and to take me fishing."

"You know the wife," Doris said. "She's a psycho."

"That's my sister," Tony said.

The waitress tried to recover. "I'm sorry, I—"

"I'm kidding."

"Young guy had ya goin' there, Doris," Walt said with a hearty laugh.

"I'm sorry, Doris," Tony said. "You left yourself wide open."

The red was finally starting to leave her face. "Well, she is a strange one. She also drinks like a fish."

Although Tony wasn't one to listen or believe in gossip, that's exactly what he was looking for in this case. Quite often in small towns the gossip was closer to the truth than most liked to admit. And the best place to find out what was going on in a town was to hear about it from the local cafe or barber shop. They were the pulse of small town America, and he was getting more than just a great omelet.

"Anything specific?" Tony asked.

She hesitated a moment, shifting her eyes about the room. Then she pointed to the two men at the table. "You two were here couple Saturdays ago. You saw her come in here yelling and ranting and raving at her husband. Then she started hittin' the poor guy.

Grabbed him by the ponytail and pulled him right off that stool there. I've never seen such a wild woman."

"Mary did that? Wait a minute. Ponytail? You're sure this was Caleb Hatfield?"

She nodded. "Sure was. Watched him grow it for the last eight months or so. Looks like the fellow from Highlander, only it's not that long yet."

Tony checked with the old guys, who both nodded in agreement. Now that was interesting.

"You say she was hitting Caleb?"

The old guy broke in. "Yeah, and not just a love tap. I'm talkin' closed fist. First one hit him right here." He placed his right fist against his right eye. "He finally picked her up over his shoulder and hauled her out the door. He was more embarrassed than hurt, I'd guess. Shoulda thrown her in the bay."

"What was it about?"

There were shrugs all around. The waitress said, "Don't know really. She kept calling him a two-timing bastard, though."

Caleb with another woman. Somehow that didn't fit. But who knows, people change. Tony paid his bill, thanked them for the info, and headed out to his truck. He sat for a moment watching the whitecaps on the bay and the trees swish sideways with each blast of wind. A part of him wanted to go to Mary Hatfield and confront her about what he had just heard. It explained more why Caleb would want to take off than anything Mary had told him, but he also wanted that as his ace in the hole. It was better if she didn't know what he knew. Instead, he decided to take a drive to The Brothers Wilderness Area to see just how someone could burn and destroy large hulks of steel logging equipment.

♦

Tony expected the drive to the Brothers Wilderness to take a while, considering the blustery weather, but he had no idea it would take him three hours. He had driven to the north across the Hood Canal Bridge before cutting south toward U.S. 101, and then west toward the wilderness. Toward the end of the drive the winds started to die down some.

A couple of miles back he had come across a road block, with news media vehicles lined up one after the next. He had no problem driving past the local sheriff's deputies, though.

Now he crept along the road, the Olympic National Forest on both sides, where the pavement had ended, the dirt had begun and was now the consistency of wet goose shit. Shortly he came across the crime scene. How did he know? He was close to the wilderness area and there was a line of cars that should have never been there, their outer shells covered completely in mud. Then there was the sheriff's vehicles—two streetwise Ford Explorers. Beyond those cars and police vehicles, in an open area cut out of the forest, sat a grouping of large forest equipment. At least that's what he thought they were.

He stepped out of his truck and sank up to his ankles in muck. He was wearing a cross between hiking shoes and Nike cross trainers—shoes that did neither with great efficiency. He pulled one leg after the other toward a huddle of people behind yellow police tape near the equipment. Glancing back over his shoulder, he decided to leave Panzer in the back of his truck. No need messing up perfectly clean paws.

As he approached through the mist, he could see the damage they had explained briefly on the radio at the cafe. There was a front loader with tires setting on the rims, and now resembled a Dali painting. What had been orange paint was now black; what had been flexible, like wires and tires and Plexiglas, was now melted and dried into a surreal sculpture.

Tony stopped suddenly when he saw special agent McCallum and his FBI partner, Carrie Jones, talking with a man in a suit. Actually, there was a lot of yelling going on by the well-dressed man toward Bob.

Before Tony could head toward his old "friend," another man in crumpled Dockers and a heavy Northwest jacket approached Tony and held out his hand.

"I thought that was you," the man said.

Shaking the man's hand, Tony said, "Jim, I thought you retired."

"Just about. Six months to go. Gotta pay off some bills. Suppose you're here to talk with Bob. He's a little busy right now. See if I can free him up. Nice to see ya again, Tony."

"You too. Take it easy."

The man half smiled and walked away through the muck. Running the man through his mind, Tony remembered Jim Pratt had nearly retired when he worked in Seattle with him. Some guys just liked to hang on. Same thing happened in the Navy.

Jim talked for a second with Bob McCallum, who then excused himself and sloshed through the mud toward Tony, his hand extended.

"Hey, glad you could make it," McCallum said to Tony, turning and escorting him out of earshot with his arm around Tony's shoulder.

"Friend of yours, Bob?" Tony asked, glancing at the yelling man, who was now nearly spitting in the face of special agent Jones.

"That fucker's been on my case since I stepped out of the car," McCallum said.

"Which one is he, Rodger or Parker?"

"Rick Parker. I understand John Rodger is a reasonable guy. So, why can't he show up? What the hell you doin' here, Caruso?"

"You mean besides saving your ass from obnoxious loggers?"

McCallum shifted his gaze back toward his partner, "Hate to do that to Carrie, but I know she can take the guy. I seriously considered drawing my weapon on him. You didn't answer my question."

Tony thought for a good reason, but came up far short of a good lie. "I could tell you a story about how I was up here looking for a nice place to fish, but I don't guess you'd buy that. Seriously, I really don't know. I was eating breakfast in Port Orchard, heard about this latest round of eco-insanity, and decided to take a drive. Maybe I knew I'd find you here."

He shook his head. "I know never to try to get a straight answer out of you. You know something about this shit here." He swiveled his head enough to indicate the burnt equipment but not enough to make eye contact with the irate owner.

"Yeah. I know that the insurance companies are gonna be pissed off if this shit keeps up."

"I hear that."

The two of them stood for a moment in silence, and Tony listened to a squirrel chattering away at them, telling them to get the hell out of his forest.

"I hate those fuckers," McCallum said.

"What? Insurance agents?"

"No. Those fuckin' tree rats."

They both gazed at the squirrel for a moment.

"Did the EDL call in responsibility?"

"Why should I tell you? You'll go blabbing to that liberal media, who'll plaster this shit all over the papers and the airwaves with smug indifference or, more likely, exuberant glee."

McCallum knew that was a crock of shit. Tony had constantly complained about the media misquoting them following a suspected bombing, or even worse, following an actual explosion. But Tony also knew the media in America, and especially the Pacific Northwest, was any further to the left they'd be halfway to China.

"I think your road block down the mountain took care of most of that problem."

"Most?"

"Yeah. About a mile down the mountain I saw a couple of junior reporter types tromping along in the muck toward here. I was gonna give them a ride, but I think they were from T.V."

"Thanks, pal. So, how did you get past the road block?"

Tony wasn't about to let McCallum know he still had his FBI credentials, even though they were out-dated and would have never stood up to close scruti-ny. Instead, he said, "Trade secret." He continued, "This looks like a lot of damage for a simple flash and burn. I'm guessing a little napalm action. Am I right?"

He shot Tony a glance that confirmed his suspicion. "What the hell do you know, Caruso?"

"I'm right!"

"You're a fucking civilian," he said, pointing back at Tony's Ford F250. "Now hop back in that prissy rig of yours and drive your ass back down the moun-tain to the land of civilians. Do not pass go; do not collect two hundred frickin' dollars. Is that clear enough for your thick Italian brain to understand?"

Tony had actually thought about leaving, giving the guy a victory of sorts. But he needed something. He started to turn, but stopped. "Listen. That Ford F250 is not prissy!" There. Now he left through the muck, the squirrel yapping away at him. He felt like digging around in his glove box for his 9mm and capping the little bastard. The squirrel, of course.

As he was turning the truck around on the mired and mucked up road, he notice the two T.V. reporters jacked up against the side of a sheriff's truck, undoubtedly bitching about the first amendment and the F.B.I. Gestapo. The ACLU would have a lawsuit slapped on them by noon.

Tony was halfway down the mountain when he got

a call on his cell phone.

"Yeah."

There was a long pause. Then, "Caruso...I told you to stay the fuck out of this."

Tony glanced into his rearview mirror expecting to see a vehicle. Nothing.

"Hey, Virtue. Put Caleb Hatfield on the phone."

More silence.

He continued. "You know I'm on a cell phone and they're probably giving me reaming charges out the ass."

"You can't take no for an answer, Caruso," Virtue finally said.

There was noise in the background. Splashing water? He could be on his dock along Hood Canal.

"Tell Caleb to call me himself," Tony said and hung up. This time he turned off his phone and continued down the mountain.

Somehow that guy was right in Tony's back pocket, knowing every move he was making. Which was difficult, since he didn't even know those moves until they happened.

As the raven flies Tony was damn near within shooting range of Pat Virtue's house across the canal. It would take him a couple hours to head north around the Hood Canal Bridge and then back down to Seabeck. But if he caught the ferry just right, he could be there in less than an hour.

He got lucky. It took him forty-five minutes.

CHAPTER 9

Things were actually starting to look up. Under normal circumstances, Tony would have wanted the sun to come out, but now the clouds were so thick and dark the afternoon looked more like early evening.

He parked out on the main road, where Pat Virtue's mail box should have been. Slowly and quietly he latched the door, leaving Panzer inside the bed, before hiking down the driveway.

People say there's more than one way to skin a cat, but Tony wasn't so sure about that. He found it best to go from the feet to the head. With Pat Virtue there was probably more than one way to approach him, also. However, in his case, Tony thought surprise was best.

The problem with surprise was that those who live out in the sticks don't like it. They were libel to pull a shotgun first, shoot his ass, and then look to see if he was anybody that could get him in trouble. Like the police. And Tony wasn't sure if Virtue was one of those paranoid, X-Files-watching, ex-military types who saw a terrorist behind every tree trying to steal secrets that they no longer had or maybe never really had in the first place. Only time would tell which species Virtue belonged to.

Not very long, though. When Tony got closer to the man's cabin, he went into the woods and worked his way around the back side. The old VW was still there. And now, for the first time, Tony could see a boat moored against the dock down on Hood Canal. It was a good-sized boat, maybe a 30-footer, with a cabin and antennas sticking up from that.

Moving around to the back of the house, Tony could see a light on in a back room. He'd use that to his advantage. It would be easier for him to look in than it would for Virtue to look out at him.

When he got to the window, he shot back when he saw a figure cross his view. He leaned against the rough-cut cedar siding, wondering how to approach this guy. To his right was a back door with a small slab of cement one step down from the threshold. Angling under the window, Tony stepped lightly toward the door. His shoes were still caked with mud, and with the soggy soil below the eaves, the going was less than smooth.

He noticed the base of the screen door had scratch marks where a pet had clawed trying to get in. That would have to do. He moved to the side and started scratching the door. This would only work if the guy still had a cat, and if that cat was not sitting on his lap purring.

Suddenly there were footsteps moving toward the door, along with grumbling. The inner door opened, and then the screen door swung out toward Tony.

"Get the fuck in here," the man yelled.

Tony grabbed the man's arm and pulled him outside toward him. The man was so surprised his eyes seemed to explode from his head. Before he could recover, or understand what was happening, Tony had him standing in the muck with him, his stocking feet up to his ankles in the stuff.

Virtue swung a huge roundhouse right at Tony's head. He ducked and counter-punched him in the right ribs, taking his breath away. Out of air, Virtue charged Tony, catching his feet in the mud and almost knocking him to the ground. Tony was able to catch himself and plant his right knee into Virtue's groin. If the man was having a hard time breathing before, it was almost impossible now.

The man dropped to his knees holding his vital organs.

"Virtue," Tony yelled. "We can go on like this until someone really gets hurt, or you can talk to me. It's up to you."

The man in the mud raised his head slightly and then slowly nodded.

"Where the fuck is Caleb?" Tony yelled.

Virtue didn't answer. Tony thought about grabbing his hair, but it was as short as his. Instead, he pulled him up by his shirt collar.

"Answer me, fuckhead."

"I don't know shit."

"Being an Army puke, that's probably not far from the truth. But you might know where to find Caleb."

Pulling himself loose, he tried his best to get his

breath. Then he said, "Can we go inside?"

The reason Tony wanted him outside was because he could isolate him from any weapons he might have hanging around. But for some reason he also wanted to take a look inside. See if Caleb might have been there.

Without answering, they made their way into the cabin, Virtue taking off his muddy socks and Tony removing his soiled half-boots.

It was a modest place; like a rustic vacation home. The furniture was straight out of a second hand store. There were almost no items that indicated he had been part of the military. Most ex-military had plaques and photos of their days of service. Maybe a shadow box of medals. Here all Tony saw in the main living area was a few photos of Pat Virtue standing next to an Apache helicopter. Then he saw it. A photo of Virtue and Caleb Hatfield on the boat, with each holding up a salmon in each hand. Tony picked up the picture for a closer look. It must have been fairly recent, since Caleb's hair was almost touching his collar. Tony had almost not recognized Caleb because of that.

"That was a couple of months ago," Virtue said from behind Tony. He had two open beers and he handed Tony one before taking a long draw on his. He took the photo from Tony and replaced it in its spot on the end table. Then he took a seat in a lounge chair and threw one leg over the arm, his eyes studying Tony carefully.

Taking a drink of beer, Tony took a seat on the edge of the sofa and then glanced around the room. There was an old desk against the far wall with an ancient computer on top of that. To the right of the monitor was a dot-matrix printer.

"You're obviously a good friend of Caleb's," Tony started, "and so am I. You must know this otherwise you wouldn't have called me twice. Why can't you just tell me where I can find Caleb? His wife is worried."

He had a hearty laugh with that. Tony waited for him to finish, trying on his best poker face.

"I don't understand the humor," Tony said.

"She's a bitch," he said. "And that's not funny. She probably wants him to drive over to the Navy Exchange and buy her some more vodka. She's gotta be running low by now."

Tony took a healthy swig of beer while he thought how to proceed. Since he had only heard Mary's side of the story, and that of a couple of outsiders, it would have been nice to talk with Caleb to find out the truth. There was no way in hell he could lie to Tony.

Finally, Tony broke the silence. "I know all about their problems."

"Then you know why Caleb wants to leave her." This came out as a statement not a question. "When Caleb left the Navy he was havin' problems adjustin' to civilian life, but that was nothin' compared to Mary. She missed the service more'n Caleb. He said she used to drink a lot while they were in, but it really got outta hand once he left the Navy. She couldn't handle not being part of the Officers' Wives Club. She had always been defined by her husband's rank."

"Caleb told you this?"

"Who else?" he said. "You go out fishin' with someone and you got a lot of time to bullshit."

Virtue went into the kitchen and returned with two more beers. He handed Tony one before sitting down.

"What made you retire up here instead of going back to the Ozarks?" Tony asked him.

He seemed somewhat shocked that Tony could tell where he was from. "I had done some time at Ft. Lewis. I bought my first boat while stationed there. Couldn't get over the great fishin' and the smell of the ocean. It's like the Ozarks with salt water. I'll never live anywhere else."

Time to change the subject. "Why are you trying to keep me from seeing Caleb? It makes no sense."

He eyed Tony over his beer as he took a drink. Then he said, "Things aren't always as they appear."

"But you've been in contact with Caleb in the last few days."

"You don't know shit!"

"I know enough to know that you could give a shit about me...but Caleb might not want me to find him for some reason. Problem is, why?"

Virtue sat somewhat dejected, his eyes shifting from side to side. He was wrestling with something in his mind. Tony just needed to break through all that macho crap.

When the man started talking, he surprised Tony. "In the Storm I killed more than ten tanks." He snapped his fingers. "Gone like that. Burnin' hulks of metal. Arm the weapons and let 'em fly. Those bastards didn't have a chance against our Apaches." He sunk down in his chair and sipped his beer. "What the hell does it all mean? Those ragtops didn't do nothin' to me. They probably had families. But ya use stand-off weapons like that and the people don't mean shit to ya. They're just targets. Fuckin' targets."

Tony hesitated to say anything under these circumstances. During Desert Storm he directed his ordnance crews to load Alpha strikes that probably killed even more Iraqis than Pat Virtue and his Apache. Although Tony and his men hadn't actually dropped the bombs, he had always felt a certain level of responsibility for all of those deaths. How could he not? "We all did shit in the name of country and honor. If they had had the chance they would have done the same thing to us."

He sat up straight now and pointed at Tony. "That's the difference. We had a choice. We were all volunteer. They were told to fucking be there or die. A bunch of rounded up conscripts like our guys in Nam. From the lowest of the culture and economic background. We had a choice. We chose to kill. That makes all the difference in the world."

Tony had never thought of it that way, but he had to admit the guy had a point. Nevertheless, it was useless to argue the point. They were getting way off track. Tony needed to find Caleb.

"Tell me right now that Caleb is not involved with this eco-terrorist group," Tony said.

Virtue's head shot up. "How the hell can you say that? You know Caleb."

"True. But I also know that people change. Remember, you're the one who called me at the restaurant and told me to stay out of it. That I was already in too deep. Then just a couple of hours ago you try to warn me off again. What are you trying to warn me from?"

He shook his head back and forth. "You are one thick-skulled motherfucker. Caleb was right about that."

Tony guessed that was hard to argue against.

Virtue continued, "There's a war coming in this country and most people don't see it coming. You got those rich bastards making money off computer software and high-tech shit buying up land around here like they're buying a bagel and coffee. Meanwhile, the ranks of the poor are rising like never before. We have a finite amount of resources in this world. You use it up and it's gone forever. Down in California they're choppin' down the redwoods to build decks on these huge-ass houses. When the redwoods are gone, they go after the cedar. We don't have much left of our old growth. The Pacific Northwest is our last battle ground. We lose this, and we'll never get those big trees back again. And think about the salmon. We dam their rivers so they can't spawn. We over fish them commercially until there aren't any left to spawn. And what for? So some asshole can throw them for tourists down at Pike Market? We need to wake up in this country."

He finished his beer and sat back in his chair. Tony thought Virtue gave him more than he expected. When he left Virtue, he was sitting down with his third beer, his head lowered against his chest.

Tony hiked out to his truck and sat for a moment

thinking. If Virtue had these feelings, could his old friend Caleb be that far behind?

It was starting to turn to true darkness of night as Tony pulled out and headed south. Before driving there from Oregon, Tony had made arrangements to stay at a local resort in a timeshare condo for a week, but he was not able to check in until Saturday night, which it was now.

Tony had acquired almost a full three months of timeshare through one of those international organizations that link up all of these resorts worldwide. Part of his payments for the past few years had been grateful people turning over their weeks in exchange for Tony's services. They had also paid him, but what he really wanted was the timeshares. He did have his retirement from the military, but if he ever wanted to settle down into an actual house, he needed the income from his private practice. He still had base privileges as a Lieutenant Commander, with full medical benefits. His needs were not great. His Ford F250 was paid off. His only expenses were his cell phone account, his internet service, and food and shelter for himself, along with a little dog food for Panzer. He was sure he could have bought a home in Eugene or Portland or Seattle or along the coast. But that was his problem. He was always on the road, and he hadn't found a place where he wanted to stay for any extended period of time. So the timeshares worked out great. He could conduct his investigations, keep collecting more weeks, and never have to put down roots for more than a week at a time if he didn't want to.

As he pulled into the parking lot at the check-in area for the Hood Canal Resort, maybe he was feeling a little guilty about what Pat Virtue had just said. He was living a life that depended on the development of large resorts, cutting into forested regions or along beautiful beaches. Guilt could be an overpowering force in one's life, unless, as was his case, you were raised a Catholic. Tony had long ago stopped practicing any organized religion that would allow him into their building, so the chance of him confessing his sins was about as likely as the rain stopping in Kitsap County for a full year.

He checked into a nice one-bedroom unit on the second floor, with a fake fireplace, a hot tub, and apparently a fortunate view of Hood Canal and the Olympic mountains whenever the rain stopped.

The unit allowed dogs, so Panzer lay on the wooden floor in front of the gas fireplace while Tony soaked a layer of skin off in the hot tub. After that, sleep came easy. But it didn't last long.

CHAPTER 10

The small boat cruised south along Hood Canal through the darkness. The man at the steering wheel pulled back on the throttle and spun the wheel around to the left. He cut the main engine and lowered the trolling motor into the water.

In the bow, the other man glanced up into the forest at the dim light glowing from the small structure. Using only the battery-operated trolling motor now, they moved forward quietly and slowly toward the long dock. On the leeward side, south of the normal current of the canal, sat a large boat rocking gently against rubber bumpers.

The man in the bow reached out and grasped the wooden dock and then tied off the boat to a piling. The man at the motor cut power and then tied off the stern of the boat before moving to the center. He started handing the plastic containers of white gas to the bow man, who was now standing on the dock.

They would not say a word. That had been the plan. Both knew exactly what to do without words.

The dark figures moved down the dock with the canisters of gas, and then through the woods with ease.

Ahead, they could see the lights from the house.

Suddenly, an animal ran across their path. They stopped in their tracks. A cat?

Silently, they made their way to the lawn, their steps purposeful. The light, they knew, was nothing more than a night light. Now they split up, one going around the side of the house to the front. The other to the back.

It took them less than two minutes to place the gas where they had planned. When they were done they met at the water side of the house, each giving the other a thumbs up. The detonators were simple devices that would be tripped once they got back to the boat. All of the devices were set to the same frequency and would be ignited with one press of a garage-door opener. A simple plan.

Back at the boat, they each untied an end and shoved away from the dock. The man at the wheel started the electric trolling motor and pulled out into the current of Hood Canal.

The man at the bow lifted the garage opener and pressed the button. Immediately, the ignition points burst to life, a ball of fire lighting the entire yard around the house. Seconds later, the entire structure was involved, flames spreading quickly and combining into one massive firestorm.

The boat crept north along the canal toward Seabeck.

♦

Panzer growled first, and then Tony heard the dog's paws pad across the hardwood floor to the door. Seconds later, there was a sharp knock on the door. The entire bedroom was in darkness, and Tony wasn't quite sure what was going on. It was always disorienting waking in a strange bed in an unfamiliar room. In just his underwear, he stumbled toward the door and peered through the peep hole. Great!

He flipped on a table lamp, unlocked the door, and let in special agents McCallum and Jones, who swished by him into the room and stopped in their tracks when Panzer bared his teeth in a low, guttural snarl.

"Panzer, schlafen," Tony said authoritatively, pointing across the room to the dog's pad by the fireplace. The dog, somewhat dejected, pranced over and lay down.

"Well trained," agent Jones said.

"Nice place," McCallum said, taking a chair. He looked like he had slept in his clothes, or, more likely, not slept at all for a couple of days.

Jones looked around, walked to the window, glanced out around the edge of the curtain, and then turned and stood, her eyes checking out Tony's shorts. She looked like she had just taken a shower, her red, curly locks still wet.

"What the hell time is it?" Tony asked, then found his watch on the coffee table. "Jesus Christ, it's three in the morning."

"Justice never sleeps, Caruso," McCallum said.

"Jacuzzi? Must be rough."

Tony slipped on a pair of sweats and a T-shirt and stood out in front of McCallum, trying to figure out what in the hell he wanted from him at this hour.

"How'd you find me?" Tony asked.

"Wasn't tough," Jones said. "McCallum knows your M.O. You stay in resorts or with friends. Besides, you used your timeshare membership for this place. We simply checked out the international registry. There you were."

"So much for privacy," Tony remarked. "Now the tougher question. Why are you here?"

It was McCallum's turn. "I'll tell you why, asshole. Your Ford F250 was seen at the house of one Pat Virtue this evening. What's your relationship with this man?"

"He's my lover," Tony joked.

They weren't laughing.

"What's it to you?" Tony added. If he couldn't be funny, then maybe a smartass.

McCallum pulled out a small notebook from inside his coat and flipped through a few pages. "You know Virtue from his military days?"

"He was Army," Tony said, a bit more disturbed now. "But I'm sure you know that from your little book. Jesus, Bob, you can't remember a couple of simple facts?"

"Fuck you!" He glanced over at his partner, who shrugged. McCallum continued. "Why'd you go there tonight?"

Tony looked around, unsure where this was going. "I told you I was looking for my friend, Caleb

Hatfield. Virtue is a friend of his from the Patriots. A fishing partner, from what I understand. I thought he might know where I can find Caleb."

McCallum hesitated for a moment, digesting what Tony had just told him. "His place was burned to the ground tonight."

He said the words like he was ordering a pizza. Oh, and don't forget the extra cheese.

"What?"

"That's right," Jones confirmed.

"Is Virtue all right?"

McCallum raised his chin toward Tony. "Don't know. He's gone and so is his boat."

Tony thought about that and remembered how he had left him the night before, sucking down his third beer that he saw. He could have had many more before and after. Something wasn't right, and it finally hit Tony.

"What the hell is the FBI doing looking into a house fire?" Tony asked.

That shut them both up.

Tony continued. "The Kitsap County Sheriff's Office should be checking into the fire, assuming the worst-case scenario; arson. Since when does the FBI look into a simple domestic fuck-up?"

"It's none of your fuckin' business what we investigate," McCallum said. "You just answer my questions. That's your job!"

"I told you...I went there to ask him a few questions. What? You think I torched his house? Why the hell would I do that?" Tony wasn't budging. This guy was trying to intimidate him, but he should have known he wasn't capable of that. Not with their past.

After a long pause of silence, McCallum finally spoke. It was a painful chore for him. "We think Virtue knows something about the recent eco-terrorism."

"Really?"

"Really! We traced a couple of calls he made a while back, where the EDL claimed responsibility for some minor offenses. He's been under surveillance. That's all I can tell you."

"No, it isn't. You think my friend Caleb might also be involved with this group."

The expression they both made gave Tony his answer.

"That's bullshit!" Tony shouted. "And you know it. Caleb just retired last year as a commander in the Navy. A guy like that doesn't just shack up with a bunch of tree-huggers."

"People change," McCallum said solemnly. He got up and headed toward the door, stopped, and turned toward Tony. By now his partner had her hand on the doorknob and was about to open the door. "Stay out of this, Caruso. Your friend's best chance is if we find him. We just wanna talk to him."

They both left Tony standing there in the middle of the night wondering what in the hell that whole sequence had been about. He didn't like someone telling him to stay out of anything. And what did he mean by Caleb's best chance being with them? He went back and lay down, trying his best to sleep, but only coming back to the strange events of the past few days. Nothing was adding up. That bothered him. What did Caleb have to do with this group of eco-terrorist? That's what Tony would have to find out.

In the morning, which was actually three hours later, Tony walked his dog along Hood Canal and then to a little restaurant that overlooked the water, tied Panzer out front, took a seat at a table by a window, and told the waitress to keep the coffee coming. He wolfed down a ham and cheese omelet and hash browns, saving some for Panzer. He sifted through the Bremerton paper, but there was no word of the fire at Virtue's place. Didn't surprise him, considering when it happened. Would have been after the paper's deadline.

Tony did a lot of thinking over coffee. Some of his best thoughts seemed to come to him in a caffeine-induced state. Yet, nothing brilliant came his way this morning. Resigned to his ignorance, he headed outside and gave Panzer some table scraps. Then he went back to his condo unit, Panzer trotting happily at his heels.

Turning on his laptop, he checked his e-mail. There were a couple of thank you notes from his last case along the Oregon Coast, a message from a woman he had been seeing in Bend around Christmas, and a brief message from his uncle in Duluth, Minnesota, who kept asking when he was coming "home" to work for him. His uncle still thought Tony's home was in Duluth, even though he had not lived there since graduating from high school over twenty-five years ago, followed by his time in the Navy, the FBI, and his special assignment with the ATF.

He ignored the thank you notes. What was he going to do? Thank them for the thank you? He did respond to the woman in Bend, Oregon. She was a special person; someone with whom he was sure he could spend a lot more time. But she did have her acupuncture and massage therapy practice, along with the inseparable six-foot python that made him nervous in the dark, and even had Panzer at general quarters most of the time. Tony explained he was on a case now but would love to spend some time with her soon. Maybe she could meet him in Lincoln City on the Oregon coast in a few weeks, assuming he had found his friend by then.

He really should have given her a call. That would have been the right thing to do. Problem was, he was past forty and still single, so he had probably not done the right thing in twenty years as far as the women in his life were concerned. It wasn't that he had a complete aversion to commitment. It was more likely that, with all the moving around and temporary duty, he had not stayed in one place long enough to form a lasting relationship. That's what he liked to think, anyway.

When he was done with the e-mails, he went onto the net and searched for more information on the Environmental Defense League. There was a lot of information. Mostly news reports about all the bad shit they had done over the past ten years. They were a secretive bunch, acting through intermediaries with no clue as to who were members and who were normal run-of-the-mill tree huggers. In a military sense,

Tony found himself actually admiring their stealth and commitment. The authorities had never caught a single member of the group. That had to be driving the FBI crazy. And since most of the EDL action had taken place in the Pacific Northwest, that was right in the realm of Bob McCallum, special agent in charge of this region. Considering his current state of mind, Tony could tell he was taking this matter seriously. McCallum had always been a by-the-book kind of guy, yet now he seemed to be in the by-all-means-necessary mode.

Checking his watch, he saw it was almost 8 a.m. Time to call Mary Hatfield and see just how much she missed her husband. He let the phone ring until the machine picked up, but decided against leaving a message, which he rarely did.

He thought for a moment, and then called the east coast, looking for Caleb and Mary's son at the Naval Academy. He checked his watch again and realized their son was probably in military-voluntary non-denominational church services. Oh, well. There wasn't much he wanted to concern him with anyway. Being a sophomore, he had his own problems.

Running out of options, Tony decided to take a drive. The weather was finally starting to clear after two days of nasty crap.

Piling Panzer into the back of his truck, Tony head-ed north. Since the coffee had not done the trick, bringing great insight to him, maybe the drive would work. There was something that kept gnawing at his gut. Pat Virtue had not been totally honest with him. Tony was sure of that. McCallum and his partner,

Jones, had been vague and reticent, to say the least. He kind of expected that out of Bob, considering their past. But he was running ragged for some reason. Sure the EDL had stepped up their activity over the past few weeks. In fact, according to the net sources, they had usually spread their attacks out, with less than one a month. Maybe that ensured they had proper planning and execution, and allowed them to escape capture and prosecution for so long.

He drove slowly along the winding road, considering every turn as he would a clue in this enigmatic puzzle. After a short while, he came upon Pat Virtue's driveway. He pulled over to the side of the road and noticed there was yellow tape across the entrance, wrapped around a tree on each side of the driveway.

Why would the FBI be so concerned about Virtue? Sure he had said a few things the night before that bordered on the radical. But Tony was finding it hard to believe that he could be involved with a group like the EDL. He just didn't fit into that crowd. Nor did Caleb Hatfield, as far as Tony knew. And if there was any one constant in the world, something intangible but certain, then it was that he knew Caleb. They had spent so many years together huddled in cramped quarters on the aircraft carriers, drinking beer on shore leave until they could barely walk, and depending on each other for their very life with weapons that could have blown them into barely-distinguishable DNA particles. All those hours ensured that each knew the other person as much as they knew themselves. No...Caleb Hatfield was not involved with anything improper. Nobody could convince Tony of that.

He got out and locked up the truck and then let Panzer out. The dog's head shifted about curiously, as if he knew something was wrong.

Checking the road in both directions, he shrugged and headed down Pat Virtue's driveway, under the yellow police tape, and on toward the burnt house.

He assumed that the locals had already been there well through the night, picking through anything that was interesting. They must have concluded nothing was out of the ordinary, or had found what they needed and moved on.

Closer to the house there was another section of police tape cordoning off what had been the main structure. Tony stepped up to the slab of concrete that had held the framing and crept through the debris. There were the normal things that survived such intense blazes—like the refrigerator and stove, and the fireplace, which was actually crumbled halfway. To the untrained eye, it looked like a typical house fire. But Tony knew better.

Moving around the perimeter of the house, he noticed three areas of intensity. Three points of initial fire at the outside base of the house, along the cement slab. Then there was also an area inside the house where a fire had been set. That was right in the main living room. What had been the desk, the computer, and the printer, was now a melted and charred pile of crystallized plastic and metal. It was not as intense as the logging equipment, so he guessed the source was more traditional gas or kerosene.

Panzer crossed back and forth around the outside of the building and then out farther toward the woods on the water side. Something made the dog stop and concentrate on an area, and then with Tony's slight whistle, the dog's cropped ears lifted up and Panzer rushed back to him.

Tony had seen everything he needed to see, so he got the hell out of there before his friends at the FBI got back, or worse yet, some local cop who had no idea who he was.

Back in his truck, he thought about what to do next. He was still no closer to finding Caleb than when he started. In fact, he might have been farther away from finding him, if that was possible. At least in the beginning he had hope of an easy solution. Now he wasn't so sure. If Caleb was somehow messed up with this group, it might be in his best interest to not find him.

Tony drove down the road toward Seabeck.

CHAPTER 11

Tony got to Seabeck and parked down by the canal near a small marina. It wasn't until he was there for a few minutes that he realized he had missed something of importance from Pat Virtue's house. Maybe it was too obvious. Maybe he was too busy looking for what was there to realize what was not there. The old VW Beetle. It was gone. Now, it could have been hauled away by the cops and impounded by the investigators. But then he would have seen tire tracks and skid marks from a wrecker. No, he had a feeling it was gone before the local cops or his FBI friends showed up. The boat being gone was obvious. Pat Virtue, from what Tony had been told anyway, didn't go many places by land. He had taken off either before or after the fire had started. Sure it was possible he had torched his own place to cover his tracks for some reason, but it was just as likely that someone else had done the job for him. And Tony was sure Bob McCallum was on the trail of that boat. The car was another story.

He was about to drive off when he noticed someone familiar crossing the road after departing a small restaurant, heading toward the parking lot. He got out and made his way around the back of a few SUVs, keeping himself obscured from view until he saw where she was going. A brown Ford Taurus.

By the time she got behind the wheel, Tony skirted along the vehicles and approached from her blind spot.

Maybe he shouldn't have pounded on the window so hard, considering that he knew she would be armed. But he did.

Special Agent Carrie Jones nearly jump out of her skin. It was embarrassing for a law enforcement official to appear startled, so Tony did himself no favors. In Carrie's case, though, she handled herself with great dignity. She fumbled with the electric window for a second and then decided to come outside.

"I should shoot you for scaring me like that," she said. "How did you find me?"

He could have lied and given her some bullshit story, but he had a feeling anything he would tell her would be smelled out as a crapfest. Instead, Tony said, "Just happened to see you come out of that restaurant. But I'm glad I did, because I need to talk with you."

She leaned back against the car and brushed a piece of wind-swept hair away from her green eyes. It was funny that he hadn't noticed how green they were before.

"You mean without Bob around," she said. "He has...a problem with you for some reason. You like to explain?"

"How much time do you have?"

She glanced down toward Tony's shoes. "You find anything out at Virtue's place?"

He looked down and noticed his shoes had blotches of black ash across them. "That's one of the things we should discuss."

She locked her door electronically. "Let's walk."

The two of them strolled down the sidewalk toward the boat landing. She didn't say a thing for almost a block.

"Spit it out," she said, her eyes straight ahead.

"First, let's get a few things worked out," Tony started. "This will not be a one-way conversation."

She stopped and turned toward him. "I can't divulge the nature of our investigation."

"Here's the nature of your investigation: You and Bob are part of a special task force to capture all known members of the Environmental Defense League. Your dictum changed a few months back when Bob finally got the government to declare the EDL a terrorist organization." She was still simply staring at him, waiting for something new. So he continued, "This new designation allows you to wiretap, pay informants, and plant undercover operatives. Bob is so obsessed with the EDL, there's no way in hell he can think straight. Why else would he come to my room this morning for no other reason than to fuck up my sleep? Anything he said could have waited until this morning."

She started walking again and Tony kept pace with her. They moved onto the wooden dock where the fairy had docked the day before, saving Tony the long drive.

"Now you need to give me something," Tony said.

"You didn't give me shit, Caruso. You simply spouted off something any junior college reporter could have found."

He stopped her by grabbing her arm. "Tony. I do have a first name."

She looked down at his hand until he removed it from her arm. "So far you're right on track. Does that help?"

"Yeah."

"Now tell me why Bob has such a hard-on for you."

That sounded funny coming out of her mouth, but he tried not to smile.

"He took a lot of heat from an investigation we conducted together a few years ago. We were looking for this unabomber wannabe. Officially I was working for him, but we had split our efforts and gone off in different directions. Remember, I was just a consultant. Anyway, I found the guy living in the flight path of Portland International. Bob was out of pocket during the raid, so didn't get any credit for finding the guy. He took a lot of shit for that. I had tried contacting him, but he never returned my calls. It was his own fault. But he knows how to hold a grudge. I was transferred on special assignment to the ATF bomb unit right after that. Not that I minded much, which pissed him off ever more."

She smiled at him. "I'll bet. So it had nothing to do with the fact that you kicked the shit out of him that one time?"

Tony must have looked surprised, because she followed up with, "I asked around. That was the skinny in the office."

"That might have been why he didn't want to work closely with me," Tony said, "but I don't think he's pissed at that. Hell, he started it."

They walked again toward the end of the pier and stopped when they reached the end rail.

"So, what did you find at Virtue's place," she asked.

Tony glanced out at the water before shifting his gaze at her. "What about the VW Beetle?"

"What Beetle?"

"I had been to Virtue's place twice, and each time there was an older 70s Beetle, a Baja Bug, sitting right in front of his place. This last time, on the way here, it was gone."

She shrugged. "So, Virtue took off with it."

"He can't drive the car and the boat," Tony assured her.

"Good point. I'll bring that up to the locals; have them look for it."

Now came the tough part. Tony wasn't sure how much she trusted him, or how much crap Bob McCallum had fed her about him in the past few days.

"What do you know about Caleb Hatfield and Pat Virtue?" Tony asked, like one agent would ask another. At least that's the way he wanted it to come out.

She cocked her head to one side. "You have a hearing problem?"

"Yes, I do."

Now she was embarrassed. "Really? I'm sorry. I didn't know. I meant...I was being sarcastic."

Tony waved her off. "It's just my right ear. An explosion that got away from us. I was a little too close."

"I'm sorry," she said, and she meant it. She shook her head and gazed out at Hood Canal.

"I said, don't worry about it."

"No!" She turned on him and pointed her finger at his chest. It wasn't a violent gesture, though. It was more like she was pointing at herself in a mirror. "I fuck up like this all the time. Stick my foot in my mouth."

"I like flexible women," Tony said, trying a smile.

That got her. She smiled for the first time since Tony had met her. It was an attractive feature.

"Can we start over?" she asked.

"Sure." He extended his hand. "Tony. Tony Caruso. And you are?"

She took his hand. It was warm and a lot softer than he would have expected. "Carrie Jones. Nice to meet you, Tony."

After a moment their hands separated. You can learn a lot about a person with a handshake, and Tony prided himself on knowing what each meant. With Carrie Jones, he wasn't entirely sure. But he did feel openness. Somehow that came through to him.

"So, Carrie, what are you doing for dinner tonight?" Tony asked her.

She smiled again. "I heard you were a smooth Italian." Looking at him more seriously, she said, "Do you like seafood?"

"I'll take that as a yes for tonight. And yes I like seafood. Where can I pick you up or meet you?"

She thought about that for a moment, as if to scan her internal social calendar. "I have to meet up with Bob later tonight. But if we go early, I can do both."

"Great. I know this place in Poulsbo. Excellent seafood. I could pick you up at the Navy Lodge."

"What?"

"I know Bob. He has you staying at the Bangor Navy Lodge. Am I right?"

"Well..."

"It's a nice place. I've stayed there myself."

Without saying a word for a moment, she finally said, "Most Private Detectives can't find their own wallet in their back pocket."

"I'm not a P.I.," Tony assured her.

"I'm sorry. I thought..."

"That's all right. It's me. I just don't like to call myself that. I look into things for people. But, as you know, my background in Ordnance didn't really prepare me for finding missing persons. I did learn some of that with your organization, but I've learned mostly by seat of the pants trial and error. More error than I'd like to admit."

Tony watched her watch him for a while—neither of them saying a word. There was something about her that he had not noticed the first few times he had seen her with Bob McCallum. Maybe his eyes had been tainted by his reflection. She was quite attractive. Even more so with the smile and the way she swept her hair back from her face with the wind. That might have been it. Her hair. She had kept it back in a ponytail, but now it was flowing in the breeze like Nicole Kidman's in Far and Away.

When the mutual staring subsided, they agreed to meet at the restaurant in Poulsbo at six.

He walked her back to her car and then went to his truck, letting Panzer out. He had been neglecting his best friend for the past few days, so he led the black beast to a park a couple blocks away and let him run. With the weather less than ideal, there were no small children in the park, which could be a problem. Panzer looked more like a bear than a dog, and his sheer size intimidated even the most ardent dog lovers.

While Panzer ran, Tony had a chance to think about what was going on with his best human friend, Caleb Hatfield. Nothing seemed to be working for Tony. He could certainly understand wanting to distance himself from his wife, Mary. But that wasn't it. Tony knew that much.

Once Panzer had chased enough small mammals and birds, Tony hooked him back onto the leash and headed back to the truck.

CHAPTER 12

Tony went back to the condo and got onto his computer for a while. He needed some raw data, and the only way he could find that was to search through a pile of junk.

Where the hell was Caleb Hatfield? And what was Caleb up to? Tony checked into his friend's credit card history, but he had not used any of his cards recently. He thought about how Bob McCallum liked to save the Bureau money by staying at military bases close to his investigations. It was possible that Caleb had simply checked into a Navy Lodge somewhere and was hanging out. As a retired officer, he had full base privileges. So he searched the military lodging facilities around the Sound. Nothing. He extended the search nationwide, for all military services. Still nothing. Then he checked his ATM card. Bingo. Although he had checked on this the day after he had talked with Mary and got all of the financial information on her and Caleb's accounts, this was his first hit. Caleb must have been running low. He had taken out two hundred bucks from an ATM in

Silverdale around midnight last night. Just for the hell of it, Tony tried calling Caleb's cell phone, and, like the dozens of other times he had tried, the call went directly to voice mail.

Tony hurried out to his truck and drove toward Port Orchard. It was turning out to be the best day since his arrival in Kitsap County. He finally had a lead and the weather was cooperating.

About forty-five minutes later, he pulled into Caleb and Mary's driveway. The garage door was up, so he knew Mary was home.

She answered the door wearing a matching pink sweats top and bottom. Nike. But the only working out she had been doing was lifting her glass to her mouth. She let him in and led him to the kitchen. From there Tony had a nice view of the harbor and the Navy ships across the bay.

"I just made a fresh pot of coffee," Mary said. "You like a cup? It's hazelnut." She sounded more animated than any other time since Tony arrived.

"Sure."

She poured them both a cup, and then she took a seat at the kitchen table to Tony's left, her hand wrapped around the coffee cup shaking slightly.

"Any news?" she asked.

"I tried calling, but there was no answer this morning. I figured you went to church."

She got a good laugh at that. "Yeah, I would have fit right in there this morning."

There was an unpleasant calm as they both fought for words. Tony broke the silence, "He's still in the area," he told her. "He used an ATM in Silverdale last night to take out two hundred bucks."

She nodded. "That's good."

There was no way to sugar-coat what he was about to ask her, so he just pushed forward. "Tell me what's really going on here, Mary." His voice came across more harsh than he would have liked, but he thought he got his point across. Her eyes were directly on him now.

"I don't know what you mean."

"Yeah, you do. You didn't tell me that Caleb had grown his hair out. You didn't mention the fights you were having lately."

"Fights?"

"Yeah, like at the cafe downtown last week. I hear that was a real brawl."

"Who told you about that?" She was both surprised and angry.

"You asked me to look into where Caleb went. I'm doing that. But you're not helping me much. I know he's gone, yet I haven't a clue as to why. Although maybe your drinking has something to do with it."

When she smacked him across the right cheek with an open hand, he could have probably blocked the blow. For some reason he let it land with a loud whack. She pulled her hand back to her chest and rubbed it, a tear streaking her right cheek. She started crying fully now, so she covered her eyes with her hands. He let her cry until the tears stopped and she was simply sobbing and trying to catch her breath. Maybe he should have been more understanding. Maybe he should have taken her in his arms and held her. But maybe she had really pissed him off with the physical blow and the holding back of information.

"Are you done feeling sorry for yourself?" Tony asked.

She pulled her hands away from her reddened eyes. "You bastard! It's no wonder you never married."

That was cold. But maybe closer to the truth than Tony expected.

"This isn't about me," he reminded her. "You asked for my help, remember? I drove all the way here to find my friend. You give me some bullshit story that he just disappeared. Poof. Gone. Then I find out you two were having more problems than Ike and Tina. And what's this crap about Caleb two-timin' you? I've never known Caleb to go looking for action elsewhere."

She quickly rose to her feet and left the room. Left him sitting there with half a cup of coffee and more words to say. He could have thought bad thoughts, thinking she had gone to Caleb's safe and pulled out one of his guns. He dismissed the idea, though, and got up to re-fill his coffee cup. Just as he sat down, Mary returned with a couple of pieces of paper that had been folded in thirds. She threw them on the table in front of Tony.

"There! That's your faithful Caleb." She crossed her arms onto her chest and sat back in her chair.

Hesitantly, Tony picked up the three pieces of paper. He read through the first one. It talked about how much fun they had had the day before. How they should do it again soon. The second letter was much like the first. Same tone and similar content. By the time he read the third, which was nearly identical to the first two, he saw a pattern that concerned him. He set the letters down on the table and thought for a moment. It was amazing how two people could read the same thing and get totally different meaning out of the same words. He glanced down at the top letter and saw the signature, or lack of one. There was only a simply scrawled "L" at the bottom. Then he looked at the top and noticed the letter was not even addressed to anyone. And each had been typed on a computer and printed up on a nice laser printer.

"Well?" she asked. "Looks like your good friend was fuckin' around on me. If that isn't evidence, I don't know what is."

"This is nothing," he assured her. "This is absolutely nothing. Who types a letter to a lover? And look, there's nothing about rocking my world or sexual at all. It's only vague references to having a good time. I've written more passionate letters to the phone company asking them to take a call off my bill."

She laughed at that. "I'll bet you have. Doesn't mean she didn't enjoy having sex with my husband. It just means she can't write for shit."

Now came the tough part, for he saw something more in those letters than she might have been capable, under the circumstances, of seeing. "There's more to these than you might realize," Tony said, his words calculated.

She looked rightfully confused. "Such as?"

"Look!" Tony moved closer to her and picked up the first letter. "Had a good time last night." Then he pulled the other two letters and spread them out next to the first. "The writer uses the exact words in these two letters. See."

"So. She wasn't very creative."

"No. You see, this wasn't a she. This is a man. Look at this." He pointed to a phrase on each letter toward the end. "The writer talks about the weather, the color of the sky, and how he saw a particular bird while writing the letter."

"I thought she was trying to be poetic," Mary said.

"I don't think so. I think it's a pattern. You have blue, green and yellow for colors; cold, rainy and foggy for weather; and crow, robin and seagull for birds."

"I don't get it."

He pulled out a piece of paper and pen from his pocket and wrote the nine words down in groups. The first letter had blue, cold and crow. "Okay, say you wanted to meet again. Blue could be the location. Let's say Poulsbo." He scribbled that on the paper. "Then you have cold. That could be the time. Meet at noon." He wrote that down as well. "Then you have crow. Maybe that's a predetermined location within Poulsbo, or maybe it means to bring something with him. I don't know. I'm just speculating here. But, do you see what I'm getting at?"

Her eyes seemed to penetrate through the paper, through the table and floor, and down about six feet into the ground beneath the house. "No. I'm sorry. I don't see a pattern. I...I just thought these were love letters."

"Where did you find these?" he asked.

"They were in Caleb's gun case," she said. "He knows I never go into that. He knows I hate guns."

"Why were you in there?"

She shook her head slightly and looked down at her feet. "I don't know. Can we leave it at that?"

He was afraid to push her. Maybe he didn't want to know that she had considered taking her own life quicker than drinking herself to death.

"So you find the letters last week," Tony said. "You confront Caleb about them?" Before she had a chance to answer, he said, "That would be the confrontation at the cafe downtown last Saturday."

She nodded. "I had actually found them Friday night, but I had gotten too drunk and passed out. I was amazed that I had even remembered finding them. Even more incredible was waking up early enough to catch him at the cafe before he left fishing."

"How did he respond about the letters?"

"I never mentioned the letters specifically."

"Right. Then you would have had to say how you found them."

She nodded agreement.

"You really don't see the pattern here?"

"Even if there is a pattern in the letters, it just means they were trying even harder to keep their affair a secret."

"I don't think so. Although these are not sophisticated codes, they are still obscure enough that anyone picking up the letter would not see anything other than what you saw. Especially one letter taken in its entirety. You have three, so I could put one and two and three together. This is similar to how the old Soviet spies used to run contacts. These are drop codes. Meeting codes."

"There's no way that Caleb is a spy!" she yelled emphatically.

"No. I'm not suggesting that. But he might be..." Tony thought about what he was about to say, and realized he didn't want Mary to worry or to speculate on something he wasn't certain was true.

But she pushed him on it. "Might be what?"

Tony folded the letters. "Could I see his guns?"

He got up and started toward the living room. She grabbed his arm and stopped him.

"You don't think he's a spy," she said, almost hopeful.

"No. I'm not sure what's going on. Could we see his guns?"

She turned and led him down the hall to the master bedroom. They went into a large walk-in closet to the heavy-duty gun safe, which was opened wide. Tony knew every one of Caleb's guns. They had gone shooting so many times, he almost felt a special relationship with each of them. He was with Caleb when he bought the .270 Savage at the gun shop in Tacoma. He had given him the Remington 20 gauge shotgun when Caleb made full commander. There were a number of older .25 caliber single shots that had been handed down from his grandfather. Old squirrel guns. There was also the old 10 gauge goose gun with the 32-inch barrel. When he lifted the shelf to view the handguns, he knew immediately that was a bad sign. There was the .22 caliber automatic Beretta and the 9mm Sig automatic, but his Navy Colt .45 auto, the 1911, was missing, along with both extra clips.

Tony closed the cover and looked up at Mary. "Has he sold any guns?"

She looked at him, concerned. "No. Why?" She hesitated, in deep thought. "My God. This isn't some kind of Brokeback Mountain thing is it? I mean, with the long hair and all. . ."

Tony laughed. "I think that might have come out at some time during his Navy days."

She nodded with relief, her arms across her chest.

"Would you feel more comfortable simply filling out a missing persons report with the local cops?" Tony asked her, already knowing the answer.

"No, no. I want you to take care of this."

He led her back into the kitchen and told her he would do everything he could to find Caleb. He didn't want to let her know that he had taken his prized gun with him. It would have only distressed her unnecessarily. Probably double her vodka bill.

Tony left her there by herself. Told her to call her son at Annapolis and explain what was going on. He was a smart kid and would understand. The problem was, as far as Tony knew, neither of them could explain his disappearance with any level of accuracy or authority.

Sitting in his Ford in Caleb and Mary's driveway, he gazed across the bay at the naval ships in the harbor. There was something so obvious he was overlooking, probably right in front of his nose, and as soon as he got his head out of his ass he would figure it out. He knew that much.

Having been pulled out of bed at such an early

hour, he decided to head back to the condo for a power nap before meeting his special agent for dinner. He had a few questions he needed straight answers on, and he had a hunch those would go over better after a bottle of wine. Maybe two bottles.

CHAPTER 13

R ain clouds and darkness loomed in the distance to the west as Tony pulled into the parking lot of the Fjord Restaurant off of the main drag of Poulsbo, adjacent to the waterfront. Poulsbo had been settled by Norwegian loggers and fishermen in the late 1800s, and was now known as Little Norway, with an attempt to look and feel like the real thing. Tony had attended a few of the Viking Fests while stationed in Bremerton, but he had never thought the small hills surrounding Liberty Bay resembled the high mountains lining the Norwegian fjords.

He checked his watch. It was a couple of minutes before six. Getting out and heading toward the entrance, he noticed squalls starting to pick up on the normally sheltered bay. On the way over, the radio folks had said a storm was pushing across the Olympic Peninsula. Tony guessed they had actually gotten one right for a change.

The wind nearly ripped the door from his hand as he went inside. He had reserved a window table, hoping for a nice view of the bay, but as he sat down it looked like the clouds and wind would bend the trees right down onto the ocean surface.

He had been sitting only a few seconds when Carrie Jones came to the door, saw him across the room, and stepped toward him. She took a seat and tried to brush her hair into some sort of order with her fingers.

"Well, we got here," she said. "But who knows if we'll leave. That wind is sure to knock down some trees."

Tony was staring at her, he realized, so he glanced outside and said, "It just started. Came out of nowhere."

They looked at menus and settled on starting off with a good Pinot Gris from Oregon. She ordered an angel-hair pasta with clams, and Tony had the halibut. Neither of them said much while they ate. Having been in the military and working with the FBI like her, he guessed they both knew that great meals were often few and far between. So those that they did come across, were enjoyed with great vigor.

When they were done and enjoying a bottle of Washington Chardonnay, she finally opened up and started talking. They had a lot in common. They had both grown up in the Midwest, found it boring, and moved on. She was still in the honeymoon phase of enjoying the Pacific Northwest. She enjoyed everything but the Seattle traffic and the lack of clear days. Those were about the only complaints Tony could find with the area as well. However, he only traveled the Seattle streets when they were not crazy with cars, and, since much of his time was spent in Oregon, he had come to know when to avoid certain areas of both states during the wettest months.

"This area is beautiful in July and August," Tony told her.

"I've heard that."

"Did you tell our friend Bob where you were going tonight?"

"I don't tell him anything about my personal life," she said, almost chastising him for insinuating something he was not.

"It's just you said you had to meet him later tonight for some reason."

She smiled and sipped her wine. "And, since I'm drinking, you imagine it couldn't be business."

"Well, I see you're packing," he said, nodding toward the bulge under the sweater on her right hip. "I wouldn't want you drawing that beast on me after a couple bottles of wine."

She hesitated and then said, "We just have to look into a few things. Shouldn't take long. I don't expect to shoot anyone tonight. Unless I get some ex-sailor asking me questions he shouldn't."

"How would I know the right questions unless I ask them?" He smiled at her, hoping for a return response.

He didn't get one.

"You want something from me?" she inquired. "That's why you ask me to dinner?"

"Well...no. I mean I might be interested in something, but it has nothing to do with the case you're working."

She thought about that for a long minute, but it seemed like five. "I've gotta go," she said. Reaching into her small black purse, she pulled out a twenty and a ten and threw them on the table before standing up.

"Wait. I'm sorry if I was too forward."

"No problem," she said. "It has nothing to do with you. Bob is picking me up out front in a few minutes. Thanks for the dinner and company." She turned to go and then swiveled back toward him. "Why don't you come by the Navy Lodge later tonight. We can go over to the officers' club for a beer."

Tony assured her that would work for him, and he watched her walk out into the darkness, a gust of wind blowing in after her.

Throughout dinner he had been distracted by his earlier findings at Caleb's house. He wasn't sure why Caleb would take his .45 automatic with him, if his intention was to simply get away from the wife for a few days. Those thoughts made way for a possible encounter with an FBI special agent. The later was far more interesting to Tony at this moment.

♦

Darkness was complete across the Kitsap Peninsula, and especially the northern part of the county, where Caleb Hatfield sat now in his truck, his window open a crack and the brisk breeze whistling in at his face.

Pat Virtue sat in the passenger seat, his eyes coming away from the night vision goggles. He had been watching a coyote in a field across the road chase down a mouse. Not even the gale-force winds could deter a coyote's appetite. "This is bullshit!"

Caleb agreed, but said nothing. They were waiting again for their associate Badger, the freaky bastard with skunk-streaked hair. He hated having to deal with this guy, but also knew he had no choice.

An hour earlier they had gotten a message from Badger that they were good to go on tonight's target. And the two of them hadn't even known they were set to go tonight. Caleb hated surprises. He squeezed down on the steering wheel.

"No fireworks," Pat said. "Then why the fuck they need us?"

"Another test?" Caleb said. "Who the fuck knows."

They had been told to drive north to a few miles west of Kingston and wait on a dirt road for Badger to show up. Caleb half expected to see the guy riding up the road on his mountain bike, his hair flowing in the wind. But then he remembered that Badger had borrowed Pat's VW Bug.

"There," Pat said, as a set of lights rounded a corner. "Dumb ass has the fog lights on."

The Bug stopped in front of Caleb's truck and Badger hurried out carrying a backpack with two handles sticking out, coming to the driver's window. The guy had a smirk on his face.

"You boys ready?" Badger asked.

"For what?" Caleb asked.

"To rock and fuckin' roll. Come on." Badger jumped into the truck bed, slung off his backpack, and knocked on the back window until Caleb slid it open. "Head down the dirt road exactly one mile." He lightly tapped the cab roof and then sat down.

Caleb did as he was told, not liking it one bit. At one mile he pulled over to the side of the narrow lane and shut off the lights and engine. As far as Caleb could tell, there were no houses or other structures of importance to this guy within a ten-mile radius. At least that's what he thought.

Badger got out and put on his backpack, and Caleb and Pat followed, meeting him at the back of the truck.

"Now what?" Pat asked.

"Give him the keys," Badger said to Caleb, his head shifting toward Pat.

Caleb hesitated and then handed over the keys.

Badger smiled and said quietly, "We have to walk about a quarter mile around that corner. You'll see." He pulled out a small walkie talkie and handed it to Pat. "When I call, you haul ass down to pick us up."

"What about my Baja Bug?" Pat asked him.

"No problem. You turn this beast around and drop me off again."

Something was major-league fucked up and Caleb knew it. "You gonna give us some idea what the fuck we're doing here?"

"You'll see." Badger smacked his backhand against Caleb's chest and headed off down the road.

Caleb whispered, "You see anything crazy you get the fuck outta Dodge."

"What about you?"

"You pick me up at the Kingston Ferry landing."

"Gotcha. You better catch up with Bozo. Take the

night vision goggles."

With a quick-time pace, Caleb hiked off down the road, adjusting the NVGs on his head as he walked.

As they rounded the corner, Caleb could see structures off to the left side of the road, back about fifty yards or so, with tall pines along the back of the buildings and scattered trees to each side. A farm house sat closer to the road to the right of the long, low buildings. It was some kind of ranch, Caleb guessed, but he couldn't tell what kind. The buildings were long and narrow and quite short. There were no sounds like chickens were housed there. And no chicken-shit smell. But what the hell was that odor? Musk? Damn it!

Caleb stopped Badger by grabbing his arm. "Tell me we aren't going to let these mink loose?"

"Hell we aren't." He swung his backpack off and pulled out a bolt cutter. Then he put the pack on again. "Let's go, baby. Time to do some good."

Caleb watched the guy slink along the edge of the first building, and he simply shook his head and followed. For a split second he thought about pulling out his Colt .45 and popping the bastard. Save the mink and shoot the fuckin' radical.

The mink swirled around in their metal cages as the two of them approached. They could tell something was wrong. As it turned out, though, they didn't need the bolt cutter. Each door had a simple latch at the top and bottom. The two of them methodically went down row after row releasing the latches and swinging the doors open. Within fifteen minutes, they had completed their task, opening every cage in all four buildings. The musky odor became more intense as the mink let off their warning scents. With the NVGs Caleb could see mink climbing out, dozens lumbering across the field in their lopping style, and he almost stepped on a few as they worked their way back toward the road.

"No hurry," Badger said into his walkie talkie. "Just wait there for us."

"Nobody was home?" Caleb asked him.

Badger giggled. "Didn't think there would be. The couple who live there have a daughter in college in Bremerton. I called as a hospital employee saying the girl was in the ER." He checked his watch. "They should be at the hospital about now, finding out it was bullshit."

"You're a prick. You know that?"

"I've been told."

Just then Badger tripped over something and landed in the tall grass. Then he screamed. Caleb flipped down the NVGs and saw that one of the mink had hold of Badger's leg and wouldn't let go. Badger was trying to scoot back on his butt while shaking his leg, screaming like a little girl.

"Shoot the fucker," Badger pled. "Shoot him."

"Thought we were trying to save these poor beasts," Caleb said.

"Not this one," he said. "This one's fucking crazy. Shoot the bastard."

Caleb thought about shooting Badger instead of the mink. This guy was a serious pussy. "Come on. I thought a Badger could take a mink."

"This is no fuckin' joke, man. Shoot him off me."

Thinking for a second, Caleb simply grabbed the mink's neck with his leather-gloved hand and flung it to the side. Badger scurried to his feet and limped back behind Caleb.

"Fuckers are crazy," Badger said. He checked his leg. It was bleeding, but his pants had protected his skin to some degree.

Caleb smacked the guy like he had done to him at the truck earlier, only Caleb's strike almost knocked the man over. "Let's move before those black devils come back."

The two of them got to the road, Badger limping more than he should, and his head on a swivel looking for any movement. A short while later they were at Caleb's truck.

"What the hell happened?" Pat said to Caleb, his head flipping toward Badger.

"Mink bite."

"That's what this was about? By the way, you smell."

By now Badger was in the back of the truck, his eyes scanning for mink. "Come on. Let's move."

Caleb took back the keys, started up, and then pulled off down the dirt road. He hadn't gone more than a quarter mile when something ran out from the right side of the road and Caleb felt a slight bump, like he had gone over a small rock.

"What the fuck was that?" Pat asked.

Caleb shook his head. "Fuckin' mink. We let them out so we can run them over." Assholes. It would be a miracle if any of these domesticated mink lasted a week in the wild.

♦

Tony had hung out in the restaurant for another hour thinking, and trying his best to understand what in the hell was going on. As he drove toward Bremerton now, he thought back on Caleb's disappearance and on where he might be. Having sat at Caleb's house looking out at the bay at all the Navy ships, and the carriers in particular, he had an idea.

The gate guards at the Puget Sound Naval Shipyard in Bremerton waved him through the front gate after seeing his officer sticker in his windshield and doing a quick ID check. He angled the Ford F250 around toward the bay and parked in a lot five blocks from an inner gate that led to the mothball fleet. Security would be a problem, but having been a sailor for quite some time, he knew the routine. Besides, these ships were only here because they had outlived their operational usefulness. They had been stripped of their weapons, and stripped of most everything interesting. Should the country need these ships for an emergency, it would take some time to bring them back to life. A shorter time than building new ones, though.

It was completely dark out now, with rain whipping sideways and biting into Tony's exposed skin.

He had an easier time getting down the pier than he thought he would. He explained that he had served aboard the carrier, showed the guard his ID card, and said he would like to take a closer look. The young seaman simply nodded and told him to pass through, probably wondering why it couldn't wait until morning. Or at least until the rain stopped.

Walking slowly down the pier, strange feelings of nostalgia seeped into him. He remembered the first time he saw a carrier up close, and how, walking alongside the ship, he couldn't imagine the size until he realized it just kept on going and his walk seemed to never end.

He stopped at the gangplank and looked back toward the gate. He wondered what that young seaman had done to deserve this watch. Even though he had a small shelter with a door, he sure didn't look too comfortable.

The entrance to the gangplank stairs had a simple chain across with a sign that gave a warning about unauthorized entry being a federal offense. Tony shrugged and stepped over the chain and started up the stairs. As he got to the top, the wind was even more fierce—the rain taking a bigger bite out of his face and neck.

Looking around, he saw there was nobody in sight. He didn't really expect anyone to see him or care about him. After all, who would want to go aboard an old aircraft carrier, especially on such a nasty evening? He slipped across the long gangplank toward the ship as if he had done it a thousand times, which he had.

When he got to the quarterdeck, he hesitated for a second, almost popping to attention to face a flag that was not there. He proceeded through a hatch inside.

Not much had changed with the outward appearance of the inside of the ship. The major difference was the lack of people moving about, and the lighting. There was none. He was forced to pull out his mini-mag to help him find his way down the passageways. He probably could have walked the entire distance through total darkness, but who knew what might have changed since his last duty.

Really, he wasn't sure if his hunch would produce anything more than a feeling of nostalgia, but his gut feelings drove him to discover more truth than he was prepared to ignore.

Luckily most of the hatches were open. He made his way to the cavernous hangar bay, crossed through the emptiness toward the starboard side of the ship, and stepped lightly up a ladder on the opposite side.

Suddenly he stopped. There was a noise aft in the hangar bay, where they used to store tractors that would move aircraft around the carrier and start them on the flight deck. Maybe he was just hearing things. He moved up the last few steps, looked to where he thought he had heard the noise, and then moved through the open hatch at the top.

If his hunch was correct, he would have some answers soon. He moved aft toward mid-ship and then turned right down a passageway that read Officers' Country. Now he tried to be as quiet as possible. All of the doors were closed, but he thought back at who had occupied each of the quarters on his last cruise to Southeast Asia. There was a row of two-man officer staterooms on each side of the passageway that ran for nearly the entire width of the carrier. Five down on the right. That was it. Five down on the right.

That had been the stateroom he had shared with Caleb on their last two cruises together. When you spend that much time with another man, Tony thought, you know just about everything there is to know about a guy. He hoped his hunch was correct.

Slowly he pulled the latch down and shone his light through the crack in the door. He stepped inside and left the door open. He noticed two things immediately. First, the room had not changed from what he had remembered. And second, the room had not seemed to change at all. The lower bunk, Caleb's, was made up as though someone was actually living there, with military corners on the sheets and a wool blanket folded neatly at the foot of the bed. There was even a pillow placed at the head perfectly.

Shining his light about the room, he saw a pair of shoes standing at attention on the deck beside a locker. Then he noticed the desk. There were personal items, not in a mess, but positioned as if someone were about to inspect the room. Talk about flashbacks. Shit!

Now he got serious about snooping. He rummaged through Caleb's old locker. There were both civilian clothes and military uniforms. He unzipped a dress uniform bag and pulled it open to reveal the breast pocket. It read: Hatfield.

That was the last thing he read until lights out. The blow knocked him against the locker. He dropped the flashlight to the deck and followed it down.

CHAPTER 14

Tony had been knocked out before, but it was always a completely disorienting experience. It was sort of like waking up with a hang-over in a squalid hut in Southeast Asia, with chickens running around the room, and a woman who looked great the night before at your side looking for round two or three, and all you can think about is shaking the cobwebs from your brain and getting the hell out of there before the cockroaches tie you down like Lilliputians.

So, when he finally opened his eyes and focused above him, he swore he was either dead or he was flashing back to his Navy days. Above him was the gray underbelly of a Navy rack, where someone had etched the words "bite me." Seeing that, he smiled and knew exactly where he was. The only thing out of the ordinary was a distinct musky odor in the air, and it had nothing to do with humidity. It was a weasel-like musk.

Tony rolled to his side. There was a battery-operated battle lantern pointing up to the overhead, providing enough light to see around the room. Sitting in the center of the room, backwards, on a gray Navy-issue chair, was Tony's former roommate, Caleb Hatfield.

"I'm sorry, man," he said. "I had no idea it was you."

Tony swung his legs out to the deck and rubbed the bump on the back of his head. "What the fuck you hit me with? The anchor?"

He produced a short metal bar that Tony immediately recognized as a hatch extender, used as leverage to batten down the hatch levers. They used to call them "bastard beaters."

"Great," Tony said, trying to rub some sense into his brain.

"What in the hell are you doing here, anyway?" Caleb said.

"Lookin' for you."

"Why?"

"Because Mary is worried."

"Fuck her! She's only worried about her vodka supply running out."

Tony couldn't deny that. He looked his good friend over more closely, and realized he barely recognized him. His face was the same; his thick eyebrows, the nose that had been broken at least twice that Tony knew of, and the deep dimples he displayed when he smiled had not changed. But his hair made him look like he was right out of the 60s, the stringy brown locks nearly touching his shoulders.

"What's with the hair?"

Caleb turned his head to the side and ran his fingers

through his hair. "You like? I fuck you short time...long time," he said in his best Asian accent.

Tony did his best not to smile. It wasn't hard, considering his head felt like his brain was swollen and trying to break out through his eyeballs.

When Tony didn't say anything, Caleb continued, "More than twenty years of repressed follicles. I thought I'd let them run free for a while. How the hell'd you find me?"

"Superior intelligence."

Caleb laughed. "That's why you're sporting the bump?"

"Well, I didn't expect my friend to bash me across the head with a bastard beater."

"Good point." He hesitated, obviously unsure where this conversation was going.

Tony decided to help him out. "Listen. I'm not gonna beat around the bush here. You've known every step of the way what I've been up to. You have your friend call me and tell me to drop it. What does that mean? Stop looking for you? Stop looking into the eco-terrorists? What?"

He ran his hands through his long hair again. It seemed like a nervous reaction to something foreign to his body, which it was.

"I...I don't know what to say."

"Let me help you out here, Caleb. I've got some former associates with the FBI looking into this whole eco-terrorist group. They think your friend, Pat Virtue, is somehow involved with them. I talked with Virtue last night, just before his house burned to the ground." Tony hesitated for a moment for a response. When nothing came, he continued, "I also took a quick look at that logging equipment that was torched up in the Olympics. Looked to me like a helluva fuel/gel combo. Not too many people know how to mix and set that shit off. Napalm isn't exactly off the shelf shit."

Caleb's face had turned from uncertainty to anger as Tony spoke. "What the fuck! You think I torched that shit?"

"You tell me, Caleb."

When he didn't say anything, Tony got up off the rack and stood in front of him. "What's goin' on?" he asked Caleb.

He wouldn't look him in the eyes, and Tony knew that was a bad sign. He was swishing his head from side to side, his breathing becoming more rapid.

Tony touched his shoulder. "Caleb, I can't help you unless you tell me what's going on."

"You better sit down," he said.

Tony found the matching chair to his, pulled it up across from him, and eased into it.

"I was at our Patriots hall one night, about eight months ago, and this retired Navy captain started talking with me."

"Captain James Webster? Your assistant post commander?"

"You know him?"

"We've met recently," Tony said. "Continue."

"Anyway, Jim tells me about this group of radical environmentalists that had just been declared a terrorist group by the federal government. But the group was so secretive that the feds had never been able to place someone inside to find out more about them. In fact, until the government declared them a terrorist threat, the FBI and others were not allowed to infiltrate them, wiretap, or any other Big Brother-type shit. Now it was open season on these guys."

"So, why should Webster give a shit about this?"

"Hold on. I'll get to that." He thought for a moment. "This is hard, Tony. I trust you, but I'm not sure you have the need to know this."

"Hey, I can fill in the blanks. Webster wanted you to get in to this group. He figures you can help them, considering your extensive weapons background. After all, they're lookin' to blow shit up. So, how'd they get ya in?"

He shifted in his chair and wouldn't look directly at Tony. "That's an over-simplification. We—"

Suddenly a faint beep came from the desk. Caleb jumped to his feet and pulled out his .45 auto.

"What—"

"Shhhh," he moved toward the hatch and clicked off the light.

By now Tony was right behind him.

"I have a motion sensor set up at both entrances," he whispered. "That beep was from the starboard...same way you came. We gotta move."

The two of them hurried out toward the port side entrance, traveling in total darkness. Yet, this wasn't a problem for either of them, since they had walked these same passageways so many times in the past. Most of the time in subdued lighting, but many times, during exercises, in conditions just like this.

When they reached the port side passageway that

ran nearly the entire length of the carrier from bow to stern, they stopped for a moment to listen.

Tony glanced back and saw a number of flashlights swishing through the darkness on the starboard side. He shoved Caleb back out of sight, and then they started working their way aft toward the fantail. After a while Tony took the lead, with his little Mag light shining their way over the knee knockers. Without saying a word, Tony guessed they both had something similar in mind.

They were almost to the stern of the ship by now. Tony took a right down a short passageway, heading toward an outside catwalk. He turned off his flashlight and quietly opened the last hatch that led to the outside. A swift current of wet air flowed in on the two of them.

Poking his head outside, Tony's worst fears were realized.

"Shit," he whispered quietly at his friend.

At least three base security cars, with lights slowly twirling about, were parked at the entrance to the pier. Two marines were posted at the gate with M16s.

Caleb peered out around him. "I think you brought the entire security force with you, Tony."

"They didn't follow me."

"Then how...never mind how. We can hide damn near anywhere on this boat. This is our turf." He slowly closed the hatch and clasped one toggle.

"That's great," Tony said, "unless they have dogs to sniff our asses out. If so, we need to find a way off this tub."

They stood in silence, listening for any movement.

Any sound at all. Nothing.

"Follow me," Caleb said.

Tony handed him his flashlight and they were off. They headed down a ladder toward the hangar bay. Once they reached that level, Tony glanced out toward the quarterdeck, where at least two men were posted. Silently, they continued down the ladder until it stopped. Then they headed forward into a large area that had once been the ship's laundry. Caleb stopped and pointed the light at Tony, before clicking it off. Now they were in total darkness in the bowels of the beast.

"We should be okay here for a while," Caleb said. "Long enough to think."

Tony could hear him breathing a few feet from him, and he wondered what he was thinking or what his face would reveal if he could see it. He clicked on the light on his watch. It was closing in on ten p.m.

"You got a date?" he asked.

"Now that you mention it...yes. I'm not sure I'll make it, though."

"The question we have to be asking," Caleb said, "is who are these people and what do they want?"

That had been a nagging question in Tony's mind since he first heard the beep and they took off running.

"You tell me," Tony said to him.

"Don't turn this shit around to me. How do I know they aren't after you? That gate guard isn't supposed to let just anyone on these carriers."

"Well, how the hell have you been staying here all this time?"

Tony expected silence. Instead, Caleb smacked him in the chest.

"What the hell was that for?" Tony asked him.

"For bein' a dumbass. You led them right to me."

"Who?"

"Your FBI buddies."

"That's bullshit!"

"Is it? You've been with them the last couple of days. You ate dinner with one tonight. They played you perfect, Tony-my-boy."

He considered that and couldn't discount the possibility entirely. What if they had set him up tonight? Sure I'll do dinner with you, as long as I can tail you to your friend when we're done. Fuck me!

Tony let out a heavy breath. "So, what if they did? If you hadn't been cavorting with known terrorists, they'd have no reason to find you. No reason to tail me."

"It's not what you think," Caleb shot back.

"Explain!"

"You are a relentless motherfucker."

"No shit."

The two of them stood in silence again. Finally, Caleb broke it. "I found my way into this small cell of the Environmental Defense League. It took me two months to make contact. I had to change my look, spend time in places I would normally never frequent, and start talking up the need for a safe environment. I found an issue I could get behind. The salmon. As you know, I like to fish. But now I started showing up at public meetings trying to save the damn salmon. Let's fuckin' breach the dams while we're at it, I said. In the end, I didn't find them. They found me. They did a story in the Bremerton news-paper, all part of the plot, saying how I was recently retired from the Navy, and how I had worked ord-nance for all those years."

"So, you're not working for the FBI. Then who?"

"They think the FBI might have a mole," he said.

Tony waited for him to speak. "Caleb?"

"NSA."

"What the hell does the National Security Agency have to do with this?"

"I'm really not sure," he said. "I think it has some-thing to do with trust. Nobody has ever caught even one member of one cell in this organization. Somebody higher than my pay grade decided the military should take a crack at these guys. My con-tact at the NSA is an Air Force general."

"Let me guess. A friend of Captain Webster's?"

"Yeah, they attended joint command school togeth-er years ago. Later they were together on the National Security Council."

Tony's mind reeled. This went much higher than he thought. He expected his old friend to tell him the FBI had convinced him to infiltrate the eco-terrorist group. But now there had to be a higher authority. Although something wasn't adding up, Tony knew he didn't have time to discuss it now. They had to get off the carrier.

"We gotta go, Caleb," Tony said, pulling his friend by the arm.

Caleb stopped him. "No. I've planned for this. Follow me."

CHAPTER 15

Special Agent Carrie Jones crouched down to the pier. What in the hell was she doing here? Chasing a couple of damn former squids with shit for brains. That's what Bob McCallum had said for the past hour. She watched her boss pace back and forth in the near darkness, his brain reeling as his eyes shifted about the perimeter of the pier the entire length of the massive carrier.

Special Agent Jim Pratt approached her, his hands stuffed into his Columbia jacket. "What you think?" he asked Carrie.

"Times like this," she said, "make me wish I was closer to retirement."

"I could use a cigarette," Jim said.

"Thought you quit?"

"I did. But I could start again." He slipped away.

A marine sergeant marched over, his German Shepard straining against the leather leash, and then sitting next to the marine as he came to a halt.

Bob McCallum clicked his phone shut and shuffled to them, his jaw tightened. "Well?"

The marine glanced at Carrie Jones and then back to McCallum. "We tracked them from one end of the carrier to the other. They seemed to hang out in the ship's laundry for a while and then moved back up a few ladders before splitting up. I left Corporal Smith at the split point, followed one man to the fantail, where the trail ended."

McCallum was confused. "The guy jumped overboard?"

"Don't know, Sir."

Carrie let out a deep sigh.

"You got a theory, Agent Jones?" McCallum asked.

She hunched her shoulders. "Sergeant, you went back and followed the other trail?"

"Yes, Ma'am."

"And that also led to the fantail?" Carrie said.

"How'd you guess?" the marine said.

"Thank you for your help," Carrie said as she pulled McCallum toward their car just outside an inner security fence.

"They had a boat," McCallum said. "Damnit. We should have thought about that."

Carrie stopped and studied McCallum. She wasn't sure if Caleb Hatfield, and especially Tony Caruso, had anything to do with anything. But she was stuck and she knew it. She had been told that once McCallum got his mind set he was like a pitbull, latching on to an idea as viciously as those teeth in flesh. "So we find out a recently-retired Navy commander is camping out on a mothballed aircraft carrier. Do we make a jump from that to eco-terrorist?"

McCallum shoved a finger directly into her sternum and said, "He's into this up to his eyeballs."

"Who? Caleb Hatfield or Tony Caruso?" Her eyes shifted down toward his finger, and she felt like reaching up and twisting it back until near breaking point. She'd taken down bigger guys than him with that same move.

"Maybe both of them," McCallum said emphatically, and then slowly removed his hand from her chest. "Caruso might not be guilty, since I did find out he had used his credit card in Oregon until recently, but he might also be guilty of obstruction of justice, accessory, conspiracy. You name it."

She shook her head. "All right. Maybe he is just trying to find his friend."

"Looks like he found him," McCallum said. "Now he's off with him. That's guilty in my fuckin' book."

McCallum stormed off toward the car, leaving Carrie to consider other possibilities. It was true that the evidence against Caleb Hatfield was starting to grow beyond benign, but she still had doubts about Tony Caruso. After all, she had been the one to discover his gas receipts in Oregon, and other evidence that he had not been within three hundred miles of Kitsap during the most recent events there.

She glanced toward the parking lot and saw Bob McCallum standing at the driver's door, his expression less than inviting. Despite his disposition, Carrie simply nodded and strolled toward the car.

Once she got inside, McCallum said, "Time to check out Caruso's truck."

♦

The small inflatable boat was powered by a nearly silent electric trolling motor. Once Caleb Hatfield got around the outer edge of the mothball fleet, he switched to a fifteen-horse outboard motor and turned north toward the Manette Bridge. The outboard made a lot more noise, but with the heavy winds the little trolling motor was not keeping up with the ocean swells—even those in the relatively isolated inlet.

Tony wasn't sure where this whole case was going. If the NSA was involved, the both of them could be monitored now by satellite. A huge relief came over him, though, knowing for sure that his old friend could never be part of that radical eco-terrorist group. Undercover or not, Caleb had been a major participant in the death of that forest service worker. Who knew how that would play out in the civilian courts?

Moments later Caleb pulled the boat toward shore and let the rubber front slowly bump into the rocky shore, where Tony grasped a hold with all his strength, the waves smashing them onto the rocks with each swell. The tiny motor worked overtime trying to maintain their position against the shoreline.

"Get out Tony," Caleb yelled above the howling wind.

"Where will you go?" Tony asked, his arms tiring from the ocean's power.

"I'll call you. Keep your cell on. Now get the hell outta here."

Tony wobbled to his feet in the rubber floor, his arms still holding onto the rocks, and flung his legs toward the shore. He stumbled and a leg went into the water to his knee. But he caught himself and scurried up the wall of wet rocks.

By the time Tony looked back, all he could see was a blur of motion against the lights of the city across the inlet. Out of breath, he continued up the hill until he reached a grassy knoll. He'd have to backtrack to the Navy Shipyard and pick up his truck. He had fucked up and he knew it. Somehow he had let the FBI tail him. Maybe the wine had impaired his judgment. His left leg sloshed along as he walked back to the base.

Fifteen minutes later he walked through the front gate and toward his truck. He hoped Panzer was all right. He had his answer in a few minutes when he saw the car parked behind his truck, its lights pointing at the back topper, and Special Agent Bob McCallum trying to approach, but getting turned back each time by a growling Panzer.

McCallum reached for his gun.

"Hey. Leave my damn dog alone, McCallum," Tony yelled as he approached.

Somewhat startled, McCallum turned and said, "How the hell. . ."

Tony came up to the back of the truck, reached in to pet Panzer, and said, "Good boy. Schlafen." The dog circled once and then lay onto its pad in the back.

By now Special Agent Carrie Jones had gotten out of the FBI car and leaned against the front quarter panel.

"That's not a dog," McCallum said. "It's a bear. You're lucky I didn't shoot it."

"You're lucky I trained him to hold ground, or he would've jumped out and ripped you a new asshole."

"Okay, okay," Carrie said. "Let's not start this again." She looked down at Tony's pants. "You go for a swim?"

"Pissed my pants," Tony said. "All that wine we drank earlier."

"Right. Where's Caleb Hatfield?"

Tony closed the back of the topper. "That's what I'm trying to find out."

McCallum said, "We found his stuff in that stateroom."

They had to also have a statement from the seaman gate guard saying he had gone aboard the carrier, Tony guessed. Not to mention a shitload of DNA, if they so wanted. He hadn't thought about it, but he had a good alibi. Slowly he closed his eyes and stumbled, dropping to his knees. He shook his head and brought his right hand up to the back of his head, feeling the bump and dried blood from where Caleb had hit him with the bastard beater.

Carrie came to his side and put her hand on his shoulder. "You all right?" She moved his hand aside. "Jesus. That's one helluva bump. Looks like the bleeding has stopped. What happened?"

Tony shook his head and let out a breath of air. "I don't know. I had a hunch that Caleb might be staying on the carrier. I got up there and then lights out."

"Bullshit!" McCallum said. "The dogs followed you to the fantail."

Tony rose to his feet. "When I came to, I heard someone coming. I took off in the opposite direction.

Then I heard someone running ahead of me. By the time I caught up, the person was over the fantail and must have gotten into a boat."

"How'd you get off the carrier?" Carrie asked him.

"Climbed down an aft hawser, over a rat guard, and down to the pier."

"Christ, Caruso, you're one hell of a liar." McCallum shook his head. "And the wet leg?"

"I was disoriented. But I ran along the pier toward the direction I thought the boat took. I must have slipped into the water at some point."

"Finally," McCallum said, "a truthful response. This is a waste of time." He strut back to his car and got behind the wheel.

Carrie looked at the back of Tony's head again. "You better get that checked out. Why don't I drive you to the ER?"

"I'm all right," Tony said.

"You almost fell over."

Now Tony wished he hadn't been such a good actor. But he did want to get her alone. "Fine."

She went to the driver's side of the FBI car and talked with Bob McCallum. They appeared to be arguing. Finally she came back to Tony.

"The keys?"

He smiled and gave them to her. They got in and Carrie drove off the base.

CHAPTER 16

W e're not going to the Bremerton hospital ER," Tony said. He was in the passenger seat of his truck, watching Carrie behind the wheel. She seemed to like driving a larger rig.

"You might fool Bob McCallum with that little stunt, but not me."

Stunt? Ouch. "Hey, I could have a fractured skull."

"Yeah, and I've got a dick."

Tony looked down to her crotch.

"No, I don't have a dick."

"Thank God. A friend of mine in the Navy was fooled twice. Got a handful. Where we heading?"

"Your condo." No emotion. No smile.

Half an hour later, they parked in the dark lot of the resort. Tony let his dog out to run for a while. Panzer ran from tree to tree, sniffing and marking.

Carrie came around to Tony's side. "I've never owned a dog. I don't even have time for a cat."

"You don't really own a dog. They own you. Take up more time than a baby." Not that he had experience in that area, with the exception of nieces and nephews.

"That's a giant schnauzer, right?"

"Carrie. You have x-ray vision?" He gave her a smirk and a sideways glance.

"Very funny."

"Right. And Panzer is an actual German. Bi-lingual."

"Panzer means tank, right?"

"Yeah."

"But you expect me to believe he speaks German."

"Understands German. Dogs don't talk human."

She hit him on the arm. "You know what I mean."

Tony called the dog over in German, had him sit, lay down, and pretend to sleep. The dog followed his commands flawlessly.

"Sweet," she said.

"He was trained in Germany to be an explosives detection dog. I was there as an exchange officer. Before I left they gave me Panzer as a gift."

"Didn't have the nose for it?"

"Just the opposite," Tony said, having Panzer rise and come to him with hand gestures. He rubbed the dog behind its ears. "Panzer had one of the best noses they had seen. I watched him work. But. . ."

"What?"

"The Germans have a different take on training animals. If a dog shows an over-familiarization with a trainer or someone else, they flunk out. Turn them into an expensive pet. Panzer was just a pup, but he latched onto me."

She reached down and pet the dog behind his head. "So, he's expensive?"

"A pup is more than a thousand. They're pretty rare. You can pay fifteen-hundred. But Panzer had already completed most of his training. He'd be more like five grand."

"Wow."

A huge gust of wind picked up and shook the large pines around them. They headed inside, Panzer right on their heels.

In the condo, Carrie took a seat on the sofa across from the fireplace. Tony switched on the gas and a fire appeared instantly. Panzer took that as a sign to lay on his pad a few feet from the flames.

"Want a beer?" Tony asked her.

"Sure."

He went to the attached kitchen area and produced a couple of Bitburgers, handing her one before sitting down on the other end of the sofa.

"Sticking with the German theme?" she asked after taking a sip.

"Guess so." He wasn't sure where this was going. Last time she was here at three in the morning with her partner, Bob McCallum, they had accused him of burning down the Virtue's house. "Why'd you tell Bob you were taking me to the ER?"

She took a swig of beer, her eyes still on him though.

"Well?"

"Can't a girl be attracted to a guy? I can't work all the time."

"So you thought you'd bring me back here and fuck my eyeballs out?"

She smiled. "You have nice eyes. But I'll leave

those alone."

"Honesty. I like that." He set his beer onto the coffee table and slid closer to her.

"You were honest earlier at the restaurant."

He thought of her naked, and images of them screwing in every possible position kept flashing through his mind. He put his hand on her shoulder, brushing back her auburn hair.

She got up, drank down some more beer, set the bottle on the table, and said, "Coming?"

He sure as hell hoped so. "You first."

Back in the bedroom, the only illumination from a gas lamp post along the sidewalk outside along Hood Canal, the light seeping between the curtains, Carrie took off her blazer, revealing a 9mm HK automatic pistol in a brown leather underarm holster. Her chest heaved up with each breath. Damn! There was something about an armed woman that made him rise to his maximum potential.

She lowered the holster and pistol to the carpet and then slowly undressed until she stood before him with nothing on. He did the same. My God, she was gorgeous. Strong but not overly muscular. Firm and well-proportioned breasts.

"Definitely not a dick," he said to her.

She looked down at him. "You've got enough for the both of us. Let's take a shower."

He thought about all the running around he had done, and had to agree. The master bathroom was attached to the bedroom. They didn't touch until the water was warm and they were both under to throbbing warmth. She ran body wash all over him, and when she concentrated on his erection he thought he would explode. But he forced himself to wait.

They finished and dried off before going to the bed. There is always an electricity with the first touch of flesh, an anticipation realized. That's why sex was always better the second or third time. But the first time had to be good enough for both parties to want to continue.

A couple of times later, they lay together on the bed.

CHAPTER 17

The Lumberjack Inn sat in an old section of Kingston, Washington, a 30-minute ferry stop from Edmonds, the upscale northern suburb of Seattle across the Puget Sound from Kitsap County. At one time Kingston had been an important lumber community, but now it depended mostly on tourism.

Although the Lumberjack had seen better days, having been built in 1952 from rough-hewn cedar and pine, the motel still had some charm, situated on a small hill overlooking the town center and the ferry dock.

The last ferry had come in an hour ago, and Badger sat back waiting for the knock on the door. It had been a long night. After setting free the damn mink, he had made his way back to the motel, taken a shower to get rid of the stench and then used some bacteria cream on the bite to his leg before covering it with a bandage. He wasn't worried about any blood loss, but he had no idea what kind of diseases mink carried. Didn't want to think about that, either. Yet he couldn't get it out of his mind.

He watched the late-night TV news from Seattle now, the report of their release of four thousand mink nearly a footnote. Maybe it would be enough, he thought.

When the knock came it was barely audible. Badger rose and thought about pulling his gun. Then he remembered that he didn't have one with him. He had left his 9mm in Seattle. No need in getting picked up on gun charges. Blow his whole plan all to hell.

He looked through the peep hole and saw the woman standing back a few feet. Donna sure as hell didn't look like a tree hugger, and that was a good thing. He hated women with hairy legs and under-arms. Made him want to puke. She was wearing black cowgirl boots, jeans that clung to her tight ass, and a Columbia windbreaker over a cashmere sweater.

Badger opened the door and said softly, "Get the fuck in here."

She hesitated, her eyes moving up and down his body. "You got a lot of nerve," she said, swishing past him into the room.

"What took ya?"

"What's that smell?" She sat onto the queen-sized bed, crossed her long legs, and brushed her long black hair over her broad shoulders.

"Fuckin' mink."

She laughed. "I heard about that on the ferry. Thought about you. Thought even more about the nice coat I could have made out of those mink."

Badger lifted the pants on his leg and showed her the bandage. "Fuck them. One of the bastards bit me."

Her dark eyes shot up. "You'll need rabies shots."

"Fuck that. You can take me in when I start foaming at the mouth. I go in now and some fuck will know I set the mink free."

She swished her head from side to side. "Just say you were out on a walk minding your own business when the beast attacked you."

"Yeah, that'll work."

"Come on, Wesley. This could be serious."

He hated when she called him by his real name. He had been Badger since his early twenties. Ever since his hair turned color prematurely.

"You still wearing your ring," he said, his eyes on her left ring finger and the two-carat diamond engagement ring.

"We're still married," she said.

They had been over this too many times to count in the past six months. "You could divorce him."

"Our religion doesn't allow that. I've told you before."

"Doesn't allow adultery and murder either," he assured her.

"I haven't killed anyone."

"Not yet." He didn't want to rag on her any more about the adultery, since he was the beneficiary of that vice. Her husband was a Microsoft millionaire who had got out just before the dot.com bubble burst—retired at age thirty-eight and spending his days playing golf—leaving his wife to play at any cause that caught her fancy. The two of them had met at a meeting near Pioneer Square, trying to save the whales or some other species. He forgot which one now. It wasn't important. Their focus had changed.

"You got any beer?" she asked him.

That was also against her religion. "Yeah." He went to the small brown fridge and pulled out a couple of local microbrews, de-capped them, and handed one to her.

They drank in silence for a moment.

Finally, Badger said, "What took you? The ferry got in an hour ago."

She sipped the beer, her eyes on his. "You told me to be careful. I was very cautious. Stopped into a Starbucks and nursed a cap. Doubled back. Made damn sure nobody followed me."

"Good job. Where'd you tell your husband you were going?"

"Didn't have to tell him anything." She took another drink, bringing the bottle up over her head. "He flew back to Detroit for a few days."

"What about that nosey housekeeper?"

"Gave her a few days off. What is this? I'm covered on my end."

He only hoped so. "I don't have to tell you that this is a critical time for all of us."

"No you don't. Everything is going as planned. When do you need the rest of the party?"

"That's why I wanted to meet you here. We need them over here tomorrow for training."

She nodded and smiled. "Is that all you wanted?"

He got onto his knees and she spread her legs,

allowing him to bring his head to her breasts, and then he wrapped his arms around her. "I think we have tonight."

"What about those two former military bomb jocks?" she asked him.

His eyes rose up to hers. "I've got them covered. They'll do what I tell them."

"You sure?"

"Absolutely. Like it or not, they were both in on the death of that forest service employee. They can't get away from that."

"That was a stroke of luck," she said, then took another drink of her beer.

"We'll need everyone at the training point at three tomorrow afternoon," Badger said.

"I'll take care of it," she said, and then took her hand and shoved his head down to her crotch. "But first you take care of me."

He nibbled her jeans and wondered if this was also against her religion. If so, she was one sinful bitch.

◆

Sitting out in his pickup truck, Pat Virtue slumped down in the passenger seat while Caleb Hatfield looked through his NVGs at the entrance to the motel. It had been nearly an hour since he had watched the dark-haired woman enter the motel room. Looked now like she was there for the night. Both he and Pat had wondered what a beautiful woman like her saw in the man they knew as Badger.

They had used a rather low-tech way of finding

where Badger was staying. After the mink fiasco, Badger had drove toward Kingston. Caleb was supposed to go in the other direction, but soon backtracked toward the small coastal town. It hadn't taken long for him to find Pat's Baja Bug parked out in front of the motel door. Then Caleb had left Pat there to keep track of Badger while he went to the carrier to pick up a few more clothes—the ones he wore smelled like mink—finding his old friend Tony Caruso there had been a fluke. Then Caleb had gone back and picked up a freezing cold Pat, hiding in the small pines across the road from the motel. Badger had not moved.

It had been only a short while with the two of them in the warmth of the pickup cab before the woman showed.

"What ya think, Pat?" Caleb asked, bringing the NVGs away from his eyes.

Pat Virtue barely shrugged. "Get some sleep."

That was the problem. They couldn't go back to Pat's house. It was burned down. He also couldn't go back to the carrier. No, they'd have to rough it out in the truck for the night.

"Who you think the woman was?" Pat said.

They had gone through this for the past hour, speculating on the woman. She didn't look like a radical.

"Don't know."

"Looked more like a rodeo buckle bunny," Pat said.

"What's that?"

"Chick who hangs out at a rodeo, big belt buckle, hoping to fuck a cowboy."

"Naw," Caleb said, "I was thinking more like a

cappuccino post-modern yuppie."

Pat thought about that and finally nodded. "I think you nailed her. Or wish you had." He smiled at his own cleverness.

Caleb ignored him. "Let's take two-hour shifts keeping track of the crazy bastard."

"Fine. You first."

"Right. And I'm an hour into my first shift."

"Fuckin' squid." Pat slumped down further into the seat.

Caleb looked toward the door without the NVGs. He thought about his earlier encounter with Tony, and felt bad that he could not bring his old friend into this whole deal. It wasn't a matter of trust. Caleb trusted nobody more than Tony. Maybe he just didn't want his friend to get hurt. The bond they had was more than most would ever go through in a lifetime. The guilt now was starting to overwhelm him. Sure the man at the forest service station should have never been there. It was an accident. But then so was the bombing run his squadron had made on that Java village. And then he and Tony had been forced to go there and clean up the mess. They had not even been able to count all the bodies. How could they? There were too many parts laying about the jungle floor. That was one helluva SNAFU. Would he be charged with murder? Sure he was working for the government, but still, a man had died. Someone had to pay for that. For all he knew, his contact at the NSA could hang him out to dry. Maybe he should have been a little more careful covering his own ass. He had gone for the expedient instead of the cautious.

The angst overwhelmed him as Caleb wiped away a tear from his eye. He hoped this was all worth it.

♦

Tony couldn't sleep. He had made love with Carrie until they were both satisfied and exhausted. Now she slept in his bed, her breathing calm and controlled. He, on the other hand, sat out in the living room, typing away on his laptop on the internet, trying his best to understand the current situation. Something wasn't making a lot of sense.

Glancing across the room, even Panzer was sleeping like—well, like a dog in a warm room.

He also worried about his friend, Caleb Hatfield. Would he be charged with the murder of that forest service worker? Maybe. If Bob McCallum had anything to do with it, Caleb would face a firing squad. Even though there would be extenuating circumstances.

And Tony also carried with him the shared lie about the village on the island of Java. He wondered how many nights he had not slept, thinking about all of those faces and body parts littering the palm fronds. Grown men were not supposed to cry like the two of them had that night. But what else could they have done? The loss was too much to bear. They had never talked about it, though. Had vowed that night to never mention it again. Their after action report had been a big fiction. They knew it, their Navy bosses knew it, and only their consciences knew the truth. They had not even been able to talk with a counselor about the incident. Tony knew that the destruction and horror of Java would never leave him. Not until the day he died. He thought about the nights he had sat in a chair just like the one now, automatic pistol in hand, thinking about shoving the damn thing down his throat and squeezing off a round. What was it they said in the Navy? Live hard, die young, and leave a pretty corpse. Yet, they had not left pretty corpses behind in Java. It didn't matter that neither of them had actually toggled the bombs from the racks on the planes, sending them to destroy that village. They had been responsible for loading and arming the bombs. Making sure they went boom. Well, they did just that.

Did Caleb still lose sleep over that incident?

Tony felt a lump in his throat and a small tear forming at the corner of his eyes. He wiped away the moisture, closed down the computer and drifted toward the bedroom.

CHAPTER 18

Early the next morning the sun was shining for a change as Tony ran his dog along Hood Canal. It had been quite some time since Tony had taken a run, and his muscles and lungs begged him to stop after a couple of miles. He slowed to a fast walk, Panzer at his side at a trot, and took in the sounds of birds chirping in the damp cedars along the canal.

He wasn't sure how he felt about his relationship with FBI special agent, Carrie Jones. Was it only sex for her? Or something more. If he had been able to read women, he might actually be married by now. As it was, though, he had been somewhat deficient in that area. Sure he had gotten close enough to ask and be asked to get married, but something had always gotten in the way. The Navy. The FBI. And now, just maybe, it was his age. Most women his age who were single had been married, and those ended in divorce. Most also came with baggage in the form of children or a screwed up view of men. What about his baggage? Not in one place long enough to commit for so many years, and, perhaps, his inability to trust others—based mostly on all the crap he had seen in the FBI and ATF—and his past in the Navy, which haunted him daily. How many women had been freaked out by his waking in the middle of the night in a cold sweat? Too many to count.

You fuck, Tony. Get your head outta your ass and focus on this case. Caleb was in trouble, Tony was sure of that. He had to help him.

Wandering back toward the condo complex, Tony looked down at Panzer. "Race you to the door," Tony said to his dog, and then took off running.

Panzer didn't have to try hard to catch him, pass him, reach the door to the complex, and then lope playfully back to Tony as if he was taunting his slower partner.

Tony held his side as he slowed to a walk. "Wait 'till you're my age. I'll beat your ass then."

When he got up to the apartment, Tony took off his running shoes and wiped Panzer's feet with a towel—the morning dew having matted each leg for about six inches.

The smell of fresh-brewed coffee caught Tony's attention. Carrie came in from the bedroom wearing only Tony's Seattle Supersonics T-shirt.

"Morning," Carrie said. Her hair was wet from the shower. She poured two cups of coffee and handed one to Tony. "Take the dog for a little run?"

He watched Panzer twirl around once and land on his pad by the fireplace. "More like he took me for a run." Tony sipped the coffee. "Outstanding coffee. You're hired."

They took seats at the table in front of the sliding glass door, a view of Hood Canal through the thick pines.

"Hope you don't mind me using your shirt," she said.

"Hell no. You look good in it." He wondered if she had anything on under it. Hoped not.

There was silence for a while as they both drank coffee.

Tony broke it. "What's the plan today?"

"Look for your old friend. See what he knows."

He wanted to tell her she was moving in the wrong direction, but he knew she wasn't. That was hard. To lie to her like that. Maybe not lie. Just not full disclosure. "You really think Caleb Hatfield could be caught up with a bunch of tree huggers? That's strange bedfellows."

"Some would say the same about us." She looked at him over the coffee cup as she sipped.

He thought he saw a smile there. "We've got a lot in common."

"I'm a little younger than you," she reminded him.

True. He was forty-two and she had just turned thirty-three a month ago. He had checked up on her.

"I won't hold your youth against you," Tony said.

A cell phone rang back in the bedroom. It wasn't Tony's sound, so he looked at Carrie. "Bob looking for his partner?"

"Shit!" She hurried back to the other room and got her phone.

Tony followed her and, instead of listening in, he took a shower. When he got out, wrapped in a large towel, Carrie sat on the bed, naked, waiting for him.

"Okay, squid," Carrie said. "Let's see what ya got."

The towel started to tent just as he dropped it away to the floor and crawled into bed.

♦

Bob McCallum had just gotten off the phone with his partner, Carrie Jones, when he saw two mink cross the road in front of his car. He had driven north from the Bangor Navy Lodge after a quick breakfast, and now sat in his car less than a half mile from the mink ranch where those crazy fucks had let loose at least four thousand of the black devils. Six had crossed the road in just the past half hour. He guessed every frog, mouse and bird in the area was hanging low. That is if the mink knew what to do with them if they caught one. They had been as close to domesticated as one can do to mink, fed only Purina Mink Chow or some such shit. Fuckin' eco-terrorists were a clueless misguided lot. There had already been twenty confirmed car strikes. Who knew how in the hell their release would affect the local ecosystem. A meeting of biologists and zoologist from the University of Washington were preparing to meet at the former mink ranch later that morning to discuss that.

As far as Special Agent McCallum was concerned, they should simply let them be. Let the strong survive. He didn't think much about fur farming or wearing fur. Leather was different, though. Cows were stupid and put on the planet to serve humans.

Burgers, steaks and car seats. Damn right!

He thought about Carrie Jones. She had not returned to her room the night before, after driving Caruso to the ER. She had sounded strange on the phone. Evasive? Non-committal? Happy? Hell, he knew she had fucked Caruso last night. And Carrie wouldn't have anything to do with him. Said it had everything to do with the FBI, and the fact that he was essentially her boss. But he knew it was more than that. Caruso, that fucker, had never had a hard time getting women. They seemed to drool and fall all over him. But McCallum didn't see why. Caruso was a damn smart ass. He was also tied up in all this crap to his eyeballs. Had to be.

Bob's phone sang a tune and he picked up. "Yeah, Jim. What ya got?" He listened for a minute, thanked his agent, and flipped his phone shut.

On the road in front of him two more mink crossed the road from left to right. Fuck it. No way in hell he was getting out now.

◆

The cell phone rang and Caleb, somewhat disoriented, found it and flipped it open.

"Yeah," Caleb said, glancing at Pat in the passenger seat of his truck. It had been his watch.

Pat pointed toward the parking lot of a convenience store next to Badger's hotel.

Caleb smiled when he saw his caller at a phone booth less than two blocks away. He listened and finally said, "Eighteen hundred. Gotcha. Yeah, eighteen hundred is six p.m. Right. Where is this motel again?" He smiled at Pat, who was shaking his head.

Less than thirty seconds later, Caleb flipped his phone off and watched Badger make his way across the parking lot to his room.

"You should have woke me when the guy came out," Caleb said.

"I figured he was going for donuts or smokes. He didn't take my car."

"Right. Good point."

"What he say?"

"Said to pick him up at that motel there at six tonight. Said things were moving forward. I think something big is going down."

"Should we call the admiral?"

Caleb thought for a second. The admiral had said not to make contact until they were absolutely sure what these people were up to. Fighting every instinct in his body, Caleb shook his head, "No. Let's wait and see what these fuckers have in mind."

Instead, Caleb decided to give Tony a call.

♦

Looking at the caller ID on his phone, Tony saw the number was not known. He was out on the deck of his condo unit. Special Agent Carrie Jones was on his computer in the living room checking her e-mail. Only a screen door separated them.

"You gonna answer that?" Carrie asked him, not looking up from the computer screen.

He considered letting the service pick up, but it

could be important. "Yeah," he finally said into the phone.

"Tony, my man."

"Hey." He looked at Carrie and thought about closing the door, but figured that would make her curious. "Bruno. How ya doing." Tony covered the phone for a second and whispered to Carrie, "My uncle in Duluth."

"Nice," Caleb said on the other end. "You fuckin' that FBI chick?"

"Bruno. My sex life isn't your business." Tony shrugged and pointed at the phone.

"I'll take that as a yes. Hey, listen. We got this meeting tonight." Caleb explained his current situation, and how they would pick up the guy in Kingston.

When he was done, Tony asked, "I know you want me to come help you with the business, but I'm right in the middle of a case. Besides, you guys probably still have a foot of snow."

"You gonna come and back my ass up?"

"Of course."

"Out-fucking-standing. Do not, I repeat, do not, include the FBI in this."

Tony thought for a moment, trying to come up with the right words. "You don't think I can tell good from bad?"

"The Feebs got a problem, Tony. That's why the NSA put us on this case."

"Understand. But not everyone."

"You think you can trust the babe? What's her name?"

"Carrie." Tony smiled at her when she looked up at him. "We just met, Bruno. I know I'm not getting any younger. Jesus."

"You got that right, pal," Caleb said. "You'll be there?"

"Right."

"Rodger that." Caleb cut the connection.

Tony clicked off and shoved the phone into his pocket. What the hell was up? He went through the screen door and took a seat next to Carrie at the table.

She stopped clicking through e-mails and said, "So how was Caleb?"

He swallowed his own spit. "You mean Bruno."

She turned the screen toward Tony. It showed his cell phone log, including the call that just came in. Although the call didn't identify anyone in particular, it was from a local exchange.

"Unless your Uncle Bruno is somewhere on the Kitsap Peninsula," she said.

Tony felt like a complete idiot. "So much for privacy. Thought you needed a court order to spy on people." He wanted to get up and leave. Fuckin' bitch.

"You mean like you looking into my background?"

"I made a few calls. I like to know who I'm dealing with. Nothing wrong with that."

"They flag when anyone looks into an FBI agent," she said. "You should know that."

"That wasn't me," he said.

She was confused. "I got a call yesterday saying someone had accessed my file. That was you, right?"

"No! I still have friends in the Bureau. They can

check without flagging."

"Then who?"

Tony shrugged. "Had to be someone else."

"So, did I check out?"

"Let's see. Former Air Force officer. Office of Special Investigations. Fluent in Spanish. Worked on a drug task force with the DEA. Made captain and two years later decided to punch out. I'm guessing you were recruited directly into the FBI, since there was only a month break between the Air Force and your initial FBI training. You've been with the Bureau for five years. Your only brother died as a freshman at DePaul while you were down in Columbia. Drug overdose.

She sat quietly as he drew out her life.

Tony continued, "Your mother and father are still living in a north Chicago suburb. Lake Forest. Nice place. Should I continue?"

Letting out a deep breath, she said, "Did it say anything about my trustworthiness?"

"Yeah. The first two and a half years in the FBI you worked out of the San Antonio office. You turned in your boss for misappropriation of funds. He was building a slush fund from drug money confiscated."

"Plus he kept on hitting on me."

"Right. There's always that. Heard you broke his nose during the sting at the bank."

She looked embarrassed. "He deserved more than that."

"Remind me not to piss you off."

"So, you gonna trust me?"

"Didn't say I wasn't," Tony said. "Maybe it's not

about you."

"You think Bob is dirty?"

"I don't know. He's in charge here, yet there has not been one arrest in connection to all of these eco-terrorist problems in the past few years."

"It wasn't a huge priority until recently," she said. "You know that."

"Still. . ."

"You're gonna keep me in the dark. I could cuff your ass to the bed."

He smiled at that thought. "I'm not into that."

She laughed. "I didn't think so. You know what I mean, though."

Yeah, he did. Maybe he did need to trust her. It would sure as hell be nice to have an insider along in case things went to shit in a hurry. Could help with Caleb's murder case also. But trust usually took more than a couple of days to establish—time that he wasn't sure he had in abundance.

CHAPTER 19

Nothing to do but wait all day, Caleb and Pat had gone to his boat tied up at the Kingston marina and lay down to get some sleep that had escaped them the night before. Caleb had found it difficult to sleep at first, wondering if he should contact the admiral and get his ideas on Badger and friends. And when Caleb was finally able to sleep, he woke around three p.m. in a cold sweat, dreaming about that day in Java with Tony Caruso. Maybe his mind was trying to tell him something.

He lay now on a bench bed that converted to the galley table by day, his eyes alert and mind again reeling. Reluctantly he had gotten his friend Tony involved with this case, against all better judgment, and now he was starting to regret that. If anything happened to Tony he was sure he couldn't live with that.

Suddenly the cabin door leading to the rear deck opened and Pat slid down the steps. "You're awake," Pat said. "Man, you were talking up a storm in your sleep."

The coffee maker slowly dripped and gurgled on the galley counter, steam rolling up into the afternoon air.

Caleb leaned onto his side. "Really. What I say?"

Pat set a frying pan onto the propane stove and started a fire. "Some shit about Java." He glanced back at Caleb. "That's out in the South Pacific, right?"

Swinging his legs to the deck and running his fingers through his tousled hair, Caleb said, "Yeah. Indonesian island."

After dropping a slice of butter into the hot pan, Pat cracked two eggs and used a spatula to keep them from spreading too far. He sprinkled a little salt and pepper on them. "Something traumatic happen there? Grab some coffee. I made it strong."

There was no way Caleb could talk to him about what had happened to that small village. He couldn't even verbalize it to himself. He poured himself a cup of coffee and blew and sipped it carefully. "No," Caleb said. "Had a girlfriend in the P.I. who was from there."

"LBFM? Little Brown Fucking Machine." Pat flipped the eggs. "I slept like a fuckin' baby. Over easy, right?" He found a plate, slid the eggs onto it, and handed them to Caleb.

Caleb had the eggs gone in less than a minute. Pat made himself two the same way and poured himself a mug of coffee. They sat and looked at each other.

"I need a shower," Caleb said. "Think I still smell like mink."

"The marina has showers. I'll top off the tank on

this tub while you get rid of that damn mink musk."

Caleb finished his coffee and then went for the showers. Half an hour later he came back and the cabin was cleaned and set up with seats instead of beds. The shower had given Caleb time to think.

"That felt great." He had always kept a couple of changes of clothing on Pat's boat. Never knew when a big wave would hit them while salmon fishing.

"We're going to have to call the admiral," Pat said.

"That's what I came up with in the shower."

"You're sure Caruso won't tell the FBI. He did work for them."

Caleb shook his head. "He knows who to trust."

Then it was settled. Caleb went through the extensive process of contacting the admiral, who he hoped had enough time to set up proper surveillance. Now they would wait for the meeting.

◆

At exactly fifteen minutes to six p.m., the ferry from Edmonds, Washington settled alongside the Kingston pier and cars started streaming off.

Badger leaned against a lamp post on the dock watching the ballet. The ferry was one of the older in the Puget Sound fleet, and about medium sized—not one of the huge beasts that carried hundreds of cars and thousands of passengers. He watched now as people walked onto the pier. Probably daily commuters, he guessed.

He and Donna had checked out of the motel at noon, taken a drive to Poulsbo for a long lunch, and then gone to a secluded beach overlooking Bainbridge Island and screwed on the grass. His knees were probably still green from that encounter. Then he had driven back to Kingston in that piece a shit VW bug, dropped off Donna at a local hardware store for a few items, and came to the pier to wait for the ferry.

When he saw the first man, he knew he had instructed them all properly. The man, dressed perfectly in college grunge, had a student's backpack on his shoulders. Badger lowered his sun glasses and the man adjusted his backpack when he saw the signal. All was as planned. Proceed to location. The same thing played out with three more men—all single and alone. He loved it when people followed his instructions.

Badger now wandered after the crowd and moved toward the marina.

♦

Caleb leaned against a side rail on Pat's boat as the first man came aboard, shook Pat's hand like an old friend, and then went below in the cabin. The same thing happened three more times. Then came Badger and the woman, whom they would now meet up close.

"This is Donna," Badger said. "The others down below?"

Pat nodded.

"Then let's go." Badger led Donna down the stairs.

The sun was on its way behind the Olympic Range

as Pat steered the large boat out into Puget Sound, making damn sure to keep his speed within limits.

Caleb moved in next to Pat and said, "Rough looking crowd."

"My thoughts also."

"Didn't look much like any tree-hugging radicals I've seen before." Although their nationalities could have been anything from Turk to Albanian, all four of the men had an intensity in their eyes that had nothing to do with pot smoking—a trait Caleb had seen in many they had encountered. Hippie holdovers or wannabes.

Once they had gotten out into the main Sound, Pat turned north toward Hansville. Fifteen minutes later they could see the lighthouse on the low spit at Point No Point. Caleb pulled the boat toward shore, cut the engine, and then lowered the anchor to the sandy bottom. Against his better judgment, Pat shut off all of the running lights. The cabin windows already had the shades pulled, so they were almost completely dark and dead in the water.

Caleb put his hand on his friend's shoulder. "Let's see what these Bozos have in mind."

The two of them went down into the cabin and saw Badger leaning over a map on the table, the others watching his finger slide across the map. Only the woman, sitting on a bench with her legs crossed, seemed disinterested as she drank a glass of wine out of a clear plastic cup.

"Is this all you got onboard?" Donna asked. "A box of wine."

"Afraid so," Pat said. "Bottles break too easy."

She raised her brows, shrugged, and then sipped more wine.

Badger introduced the four men there as Alpha, Bravo, Charlie, and Delta. Caleb noticed the first two men were fine with their moniker, but the last two seemed to cringe with their fake names. Then the skunk-haired leader named the two of them Colt and Hawk.

"All right," Badger said. "Time to get things rolling." He pointed to the map, a detailed representation of the Puget Sound area from the Canadian border in the north to Olympia in the south. It was mostly a marine map, with ocean depths clearly indicated. "Hawk, where's the worst place you'd want to scuttle your boat?"

Pat's eyes shifted to Caleb and then to the map. "Nowhere."

"Just as an example," Badger said. "Humor me."

Pat looked over the map, pointed at a section, and said, "Here."

"The Strait of Juan de Fuca?" Badger butchered the name.

"Yeah," Pat said. "Juan de Fuca." He pronounced it properly.

"Why?"

"Least sheltered. High waves. High tides. It can be treacherous. Is this another test?"

Badger ignored him. "What about here?" He pointed to a place halfway between Seattle and Bainbridge Island."

Pat shook his head. "There's a lot of marine traffic there. Other than that, it's not a big problem."

Wondering what in the hell was going on, Caleb looked around the small cabin at the faces. No help there.

Badger pulled out a brochure from inside his coat and flipped through to a page that was bent over. "What you think of this?"

It was a photo of the largest ferry in the Washington state fleet. Below that was a table with running times to and from various locations.

"What about it?" Pat said.

Badger looked at his four men, who quickly came to the side of Pat and Caleb, one on each arm.

"What the fuck," Caleb said, thinking about going for his Colt .45. Before he could, though, one of the men slid his hand inside his jacket and pulled out the gun. The other one patted him down for any other weapons. When he found Caleb's phone, he took that. The other two did the same to Pat, taking his phone. He didn't carry a gun, but did have a diver's knife strapped to his right calf. One man took the phones and weapons above to the outer deck. He came back in less than a minute, and Caleb guessed his gun was now sitting on the sandy bottom. Damn it. His favorite piece.

"Now," Badger said, "here's the plan. This ferry goes down here. That's Alpha Cell." He pointed to a point on the map. "By the time rescue craft can get to the scene, this tub will be at the bottom of the Sound."

"Just a fuckin' minute," Caleb said. "What does this have to do with the environment?"

Badger smiled and said, "You know how much

these things pollute? Not to mention all the cars onboard. They're an abomination."

"So what about the twenty-five hundred people who might just be on the ferry?" Caleb asked.

Shrugging, Badger said, "I guess they shouldn't be on there that day. Casualties of war."

Caleb tried hard to calm himself. These fuckers were crazy, but he couldn't protest. Not now. He simply nodded agreement.

Badger went back to the map. "Bravo Cell will stall a car here," he said, pointing to I-5 along Boeing Field. "Blow it remotely at the right moment. Meanwhile, we've got another car down here." His finger shifted to I-5 at Federal Way. "We blow that one ten minutes later."

Caleb played along. "Brilliant. Traffic will be in chaos. What about Charlie and Delta?"

Badger smirked again. "Charlie will be at SeaTac. Only they will know their mission there. Delta will take out trains. Amtrak and freight."

Pat looked like he was in shock. But he said, "How can they do that?"

Badger looked at Caleb and said, "That's where your good friend Colt comes in. He will train each of these cell leaders, who will head up each team."

"That's it?" Caleb asked. "We don't have to help with the actual bombing?"

"We'll need your help with this boat," Badger said. "But once you train these four men, most of your work will be done."

"Where will you get enough explosives for this?"

♦

It had taken Tony most of the day to round up a boat big enough to take out onto Puget Sound. He had finally rented an 18-foot Lund with a ninety-horse Merc outboard motor, downriggers, and fishing poles attached to those, making them look like a couple of folks out fishing for salmon. Carrie Jones sat in a forward swivel chair, parabolic microphone extended from her right arm, trying to get closer to their target boat in the distance, while Tony sat at the console keeping them stationary with a small electric trolling motor as he viewed Virtue's boat through NVGs. Panzer lay at Tony's feet, his head propped onto his tennis hikers.

"Picking up anything at all," Tony said softly. The wind was starting to pick up. That, and the fact that his parabolic mic was not the most sensitive on the market, made it almost impossible to hear what was going on inside the boat.

"No. Can you get any closer?"

"Not without them catching us." As they sat in the Kingston harbor earlier watching Virtue's boat, they had both been somewhat surprised to see so many people show up there. They had guessed right, at least, that the meeting would move to some other location. Hence the boat.

"What did that guy just throw overboard?" she asked.

Tony wasn't totally sure about that. "I don't know. Maybe a gun. Looked like more than one thing, though."

He saw movement on the boat just as Carrie said, "Got something going down."

Two men appeared on the deck of Virtue's boat, one got behind the wheel and cranked up the engine. The other stood to his side.

"They're lifting the anchor," Carrie said.

Watching through the NVGs, Tony saw bubbles churn up at the stern, meaning the boat was moving out. Tony tried to start the Merc but it cranked and wouldn't turn over.

Carrie put down the parabolic and came to Tony's side. "What's going on?"

Tony tried again. Nothing. "Shit!" He waited a couple of seconds and then turned over the engine again, letting it crank for twenty seconds before it finally started. Once it got going, he powered up and headed out after Virtue's boat. They were at least a mile ahead of them, though, and moving out at a good pace.

They passed the Point No Point lighthouse, its beacon rotating on them and exposing them for a second.

"Can you catch them?" she yelled in the wind.

"Don't think so."

A few minutes later the lights of Virtue's boat disappeared. Was he actually cruising blind? No. He had rounded a spit.

"Where'd they go?" She took the NVGs from Tony and gazed ahead on the Sound.

"They went around the point into Hood Canal," Tony said. "That's a good thing. If they had gone out toward Vancouver Island and the Strait of Juan de Fuca, we woulda been de fucked." He didn't trust this boat out in that open water.

Moments later they also rounded the point and cruised into Hood Canal, the lights on the floating Hood Canal Bridge miles ahead in the distance. Yet, he was still able to see the rear running lights on Virtue's boat. Instead of crossing under the bridge, though, Virtue angled to the left through a narrow passage by Port Gamble.

"Got them now," Tony said. "That's a long bay. We can wait for them or go in after them." He slowed the boat when he reached the narrow passage and could barely see the lights ahead, where Virtue had seemed to be moving slowly along the eastern shore of the bay.

Carrie moved closer to Tony and said, "I didn't have time to tell you, but that was Virtue and Hatfield on the deck." She fumbled with the recorder, backing up the tape until she got to the point she was looking for, and then handed over the headset to Tony.

"What?"

"Just listen." She clicked play.

Tony listened to his friend on the tape, along with a group of cussing by Pat Virtue. When the tape went blank, Tony handed the headset back to Carrie. "He knew we were there."

"He's a smart guy. Who's Bertha?"

"That's his Colt forty-five. He wanted us to know they had dumped it overboard. But he's also without any communication. They dumped both of their cell phones and disabled the boat's comm."

"I wish he could have told us more."

Yet, he had told them enough. "He said they

weren't tree huggers, but they were crazy fucks. That mean anything to you?"

She shook her head.

Moving the boat farther into the bay, Tony wasn't sure what he should do. For all he knew, these radical bastards were setting both Caleb and Virtue up for something big. But what?

That was the problem. If Caleb had wanted Tony to come rushing in like the cavalry, he would have said so. All he had to say was the key phrase, "Hostile Environment." Say that and Tony would bring in the entire Navy. Something was up, but Caleb wasn't ready to end this.

CHAPTER 20

B ob McCallum, FBI special agent in charge
of the Seattle office, walked through the
darkness along Alaskan Way two blocks
from Pioneer Square and a block south of the passenger ferry terminal. He stopped and glanced at a
small gaggle of people hanging out on the sidewalk—young folks smoking pot and passing it from
one to the next. Bunch of lost fuckers, he thought.
Part of him wanted to cross the street and shove his
gun down their throats. Make them understand how
they were ruining their lives. The other part, the part
that didn't give a shit, hoped they would keep it up
and die a slow death, wasting away until their brains
were fried. Screw it. That was the problem of the
local cops. He had bigger fish to fry.

He thought about Carrie Jones, and knew she was
probably with Caruso at this moment. More than
likely screwing the bastard also. What the fuck did
she see in him? Again, he wasn't her keeper. As long
as it didn't interfere with her work.

Focus Bob. Less than an hour ago he had gotten a

call to meet someone here. Someone who would reveal the mole that had alluded him for the past few years. Although he had an idea the person had to work in his office, the voice had been electronically altered. No way in hell to tell who had made it. No way in hell to know who he was looking for, or even if the caller was himself—perhaps herself—the actual mole. He imagined he was being watched now.

Stepping lightly across the busy highway, McCallum moved out onto a platform overlooking Elliot Bay, the darkness broken only by warehouse lights to the south and distant house lights on Vashon and Bainbridge Islands. As he had passed the pot smokers, he had taken in a whiff of the sweet odor. In his youth he might have been able to identify the origin of the substance, but now he was far out of tune to all the new product. Maybe he had been too caught up in the office. Perhaps that's why he had not been able to find the mole. He could see the big picture, yet the micro management had always alluded him.

When McCallum saw the shorter figure appear along the wall some twenty feet away, dressed in a long coat nearly to the cement surface, he felt his gun on his right hip with his elbow and remembered he had chambered a round in the car a few minutes ago. His contact wore a black knit hat pulled down over his ears. Wait for it, Bob. Wait for the signal.

His contact turned his back and then there was a green glow from a watch light just to the left of the man's head. Left handed, McCallum thought. He racked his brain now thinking about who he knew that was left handed. Come on, asswipe, you're a trained observer. He'd know soon enough.

McCallum turned on his own watch light and then walked toward the contact.

"That's close enough," came a man's voice.

McCallum stopped and knew instantly who it was. "You?"

"I've got what you need." He slid his hand out of his pocket.

By the time McCallum registered the gun in his brain, the flash burst into his retina, he felt a sharpness in his chest, and he found himself falling back to the cement surface. He couldn't breath. The vest had saved his life but he couldn't pull in any air. Laying there on his back, he thought about the blast, or lack of one. A silencer?

The man appeared above McCallum. "Too bad they don't make a bullet-proof face mask."

The second bullet entered McCallum's left eye socket, scrambled his brain, and blew a hole through the back of his skull. The third bullet, fully unnecessary, exploded through the man's crotch and obliterated his left testicle.

Glancing about the area, certain he had not been seen, the man slid his gun into his coat pocket and slowly drifted out to Alaskan Way.

♦

Aboard Virtue's boat, occasionally the half moon would appear from the swirling clouds, giving Caleb a view of the shore less than a hundred yards away. They had cruised down the narrow bay to an isolated inlet, shut down the engine, and dropped anchor. Then Badger, along with the total blond-haired man, had taken the inflatable boat to shore. Why? Caleb had no clue.

Pat Virtue came up from below deck and leaned against the console. "Fuckers are drinking all my wine."

"Yeah. Let's hope they all get wasted and fall over-board." Caleb listened carefully and said, "Listen. These bastards are nuts. We gotta find a way out of this."

"Not yet. The admiral has us tagged by GPS. We need to do the same with them." He shifted his head toward the cabin door.

Pat was more confident than normal, Caleb thought. Maybe he shouldn't worry about these idiots. After all, he had the power in this arrange-ment. They needed his bomb skills. But what about after the bombs were built? Yeah, that would be a problem. Especially since he no longer had his Colt.

"We don't have one complete name," Caleb said.

Pat smiled and pulled something from his coat pocket. A driver's license. "Donna Kabek," he read. "Hmm...Mercer Island address. Must be just down the road from Bill Gates."

Caleb grabbed the license from Pat and looked at it. "How'd you get this?"

Pat took back the license and slid it from one hand to the next like a magician. "Little slight of hand. She went to the head and left her purse on the bench."

"What about those other assholes?"

Pat's disposition changed to more somber. "That

could be a problem. If they're smart, they won't have ID on them. But I'm guessing they do."

Caleb moved closer and made his voice softer. "I don't think they have any plan to let us go. Not once they get what they want."

"Maybe so. But, of course, we'll still get the last word of this when they try to set off the bombs."

There was always that.

The sound of the small inflatable splashing against the water, along with the quiet little electric motor, came toward Virtue's boat, shutting the both of them up in a hurry. When the inflatable dingy came up to the stern platform, Pat took the line and then helped the two men aboard. They were carrying a plastic waterproof box. All of them went below to the cabin.

Once down below deck, Badger opened the plastic box and glanced inside. "Everything you asked for," he said to Caleb.

The blond man started to reach inside, but Caleb slapped his hand away. "Don't fuckin' touch shit until I tell you."

The man looked at Badger for help, but he only shrugged his shoulders.

Running his hands through a few items, Caleb knew immediately there was something wrong. He had given the man a list of actuators, electrical circuit boards and timing devices, along with back ups. Not expecting the man to come through with his first choices, since they were all military issue, he had thrown them in just for the hell of it. However, every one of the items he had asked for were here. All military equipment.

"How'd you get all of these?" Caleb asked Badger. He looked at the radical bastard for any sign of lying, but all he got was his normal smirk.

"You ask and I get," Badger said. "That's all you need to know. Being ex-military you understand operational security."

Yeah, he sure as hell did. Better than this fucker. Caleb also knew that every item in the box could be traced back to not only the military source, but also the name of the person in the factory who had put the item together. No need to worry the man with that information, though.

"Out-fucking-standing," Caleb finally said. "Hell of a deal. Time to learn how to blow some shit up."

The four men stood by eagerly waiting, a smile on every face.

Caleb would eventually need some time to make a few changes to the timing boards. He guessed he'd need about five ten minutes with each. He couldn't simply make them blow up when they connected the wires wrong because Caleb could be standing right next to the bastards. No, he'd have to get a little creative. That's the way he liked it anyway. Now he smiled right alone with the others.

♦

"You getting anything over that mic?" Tony asked Carrie quietly. A whisper. They had gone downwind of Virtue's boat, hoping to let the wind help with the sound. Now they were nearly a hundred yards away, Tony using the boat's anchor from the bow to keep them relatively close. But he thought maybe the anchor was dragging across the bottom with the strong outward tide.

"A couple of words here and there," she said. "Call your buddy and tell him to speak up."

"They dumped his phone over the side," he reminded her.

"Right."

Panzer suddenly shot to a sitting position and whined, his massive head just inches from Tony's face.

"What?" Tony said to Panzer. "You gotta take a piss now? You'll have to hold it."

"I've gotta go, too," Carrie said.

"Is this where you get penis envy?"

"I think so."

Panzer nudged his nose against Tony and then looked to his side.

"I can't help you right now," Tony said more emphatically.

Tony looked back to the south to make sure they had not drifted away from the small point of cedars and fir trees that would block their silhouette whenever the half moon poked out from the clouds. They were still all right, although a little closer to shore than a few minutes ago.

"What?"

"We're sliding a bit," Tony said.

Suddenly there was a loud splash just out from the bow, startling Carrie and almost knocking her from her seat.

"Salmon," Tony said to her, and he helped her back

into her chair.

She said, "Did I tell you I hate the ocean?" When he didn't answer, she continued, "Creatures hanging out down there give me the creeps."

"So you put in for Seattle?"

"Hey, gotta confront your problems. Hang on."

"What?"

She turned the parabolic mic toward the center of the long bay. "Another boat heading down the inlet. About a half mile out."

Great. That's all they needed. "Must have been what Panzer was trying to tell me." Tony put the NVGs to his eyes and noticed two things. First, the boat was running without lights. And second, the boat was as gray as the night. He had seen that type of boat in his Navy days, used exclusively by SEALS.

"What the fuck is going on?" Tony whispered.

"Tell me."

"It's a Navy Mark Five, eighty-two foot, special ops boat. Fucker'll do better than forty-five knots. Holds a five-man SEAL team."

She pulled the NVGs from Tony and looked at the sleek boat cut through the light chop like a knife through pudding. "Coincidence?"

Tony laughed. "I don't believe in coincidences like this." Now his only thoughts were what in the hell those on that boat had in mind. They would be equipped with not only NVGs like his—only better—but also Forward-looking Infra-red, or FLIR, that would not only pick up those on Virtue's boat, but also them. The Mark V would also have fifty caliber guns, not to mention 40mm weapons, 7.62 gatling guns and 25mm guns. Probably shoulder-mounted missiles also. Enough fire power to take out a damn destroyer.

CHAPTER 21

The plan was as simple as the minds who had conceived it. Caleb stood over the cabin table, his finger flowing from point to point around the Puget Sound area. He heard the boat outside but pretended not to.

"What's that?" Badger asked, his ears turning toward the bulkhead.

Caleb thought fast and then handed his NVGs to Pat. "Take a look."

Pat read his eyes and left in a hurry.

"Now," Caleb said. "The two of you are truck drivers?"

Two men nodded together.

"Great. So then you must be on the Tacoma Narrows Bridge, one on each end at precisely the same time. Coordinate by cell phone." Caleb pointed to the center of the high bridge that divided Tacoma and the Kitsap Peninsula. "One eastbound and one westbound." Without saying it out loud, Caleb had to admit that plan made a lot of sense.

"We stay in the left lane?" the one with the blond

hair asked.

Badger ignored the sound outside, which had passed, and came to the table. "Right. Each of you will be in the left lane. You'll see each other. Slow down to almost nothing, taking up more than one lane, and then turn to the right and block all the traffic. Before anyone knows what's happening, you get the hell out of there."

"Going where?" It was the blond again.

Caleb said, "This is not a one-way trip. You'll parachute over the side. One here and the other here."

"That's why I've had the both of you take lessons," Badger instructed.

The two men smiled with that.

Caleb pulled out the nautical map and said, "Then a boat will pick you up here."

The blond man was confused. "Won't the bridge fall on us?"

Badger smiled. "No. The wind is strong through the Narrows. It will blow you to the south. The boat should pick you up here." He pointed to a spot down the Narrows. "Then you'll escape into Carr Inlet. You'll get the location later."

"But the bridge will drop," the blond one said.

Badger looked at Caleb. "Absolutely. The tankers will blow simultaneously from a Semtex charge, sending burning fuel outward onto the cars, which should set off secondary explosions. More importantly, though, the burning fuel through the hole it blows in the concrete will warp the steel beams. The weight from the cars will do the rest."

Caleb looked at each of their faces and knew if it

ever came to that, which it would not, the two truck drivers would be more than surprised when both trucks failed to blow. And, of course, waiting for them at the bottom would be his friends from the NSA. Did he have enough for the NSA to turn everything over to the FBI, though? And what about the mole there?

♦

No longer did the clouds open for them, the moon showing itself. Tony and Carrie hunkered down into the open boat as the first rain started to pound them, the drops first large and sporadic and then turning into a full-out downpour. Tony thought about the monsoons of Southeast Asia, only this was much colder. He pulled the hood of his rain coat tight around his face. Panzer had enough sense to curl himself into a ball around Tony's chair, protected partially by Tony's body.

"Have you seen that Navy boat?" Carrie asked him.

"It could be driving right up our ass," Tony said. "It's an all-weather craft. They could be inside smokin' and jokin' right now, watching our heat signature go from orange to blue with this crap."

"What do we do?"

That was the problem. If they moved in now, there was no way of knowing if Caleb and Pat had enough on these people to implicate them in anything—other than the fire at the forest service headquarters and setting a bunch of mink free. But Caleb had thought there was much more, and he was only being tested for a bigger hit. What did these crazy bastards want?

Pulling his cell phone from an inside pocket, Tony punched in a number, loosened his hood, and shoved the cell to his ear and waited.

"Who you calling?" Carrie asked. Her teeth chattered as she spoke.

"Bob."

"Why?"

"I think it's time to bring him in to this."

Either she was too cold to protest, or she actually agreed with him. She sunk down lower in the boat, her arms held tight to her soaked body.

The phone kept ringing. Tony was about to hang up, when he heard a faint click on the other end.

"Bob?" Tony said a little louder than he wanted.

Nothing.

"How can I help you?"

It wasn't Bob McCallum. "Who is this?" Tony looked at Carrie, confused. He thought he recognized the voice. "I said, who the fuck is this?"

"Who is this?" The man said.

Tony clicked off the phone and looked at it for a moment. Had he called the wrong number. It was dark, but his numbers on his cell glowed. He tried the number again. This time the man picked up on the second ring.

"All right," Tony said. "I'm looking for Bob. You've obviously got his phone. But where the hell is he?"

Pause on the other end. "Is this Tony Caruso?"

Okay. This was strange. "Brad? Is this Brad Hedstrom?"

"Yeah."

Hedstrom was a detective with the Seattle Police. Homicide. "Did I call your number by mistake?" Tony asked him.

"No. This is Bob McCallum's phone." A long pause. "Bob's dead."

"What! How?"

The homicide detective explained how he had caught the case and they were bagging Bob when his phone, already in an evidence bag, went off.

Carrie Jones wasn't sure what was going on, but she didn't seem too worried either, her body in a full-out shake fest now.

"I'm with Bob's partner right now," Tony said. He listened for a while, keeping his eyes on Carrie. Finally he said to the detective, "Anything I can do to help, just ask the question."

"Where are you now?" the detective asked Tony. "You sound like you're outside."

"I'm on a frickin' boat down an inlet off Hood Canal freezing my ass off."

"Could what you're looking into have anything to do with Bob's murder?"

"Don't know. Maybe." Tony didn't want to mention everything to the detective. "Bob was looking into the forest service fire and the mink release."

Pause. "Doesn't sound like something the enviro-crazies would do."

"Maybe. I'll get back with you tomorrow." Tony flipped his phone shut and zipped it into his jacket.

"Who was that?" Carrie asked him.

There was no good way to say someone was dead.

Only the direct way. "Bob was murdered in Seattle tonight."

From what Tony could see of her face, it was as cold as the wind-whipped rain. "How?" she forced out and then gulped.

Tony told her. When he was done, he said, "We need to haul every one of these fuckers in and interrogate the shit outta them."

He saw her head nod agreement.

"You wearing your Kevlar?" Tony asked her.

She tapped her chest. "Yep."

"Good. Then let's go." He explained the plan to her as he pulled the anchor into the boat. They would use the electric trolling motor, coming in slow and quiet. She would tie up to the stern of Virtue's boat and wait for him to come aboard. With any luck, they'd catch them with their pants down.

Tony turned over the handle on the electric motor, and even at full throttle they were barely making progress toward the boat, the waves and wind nearly holding them in place. This would take longer than expected. He only hoped the battery had enough power.

♦

On Virtue's boat, everyone was down below in the warmth of the cabin. Pat had come down a while ago, saying a fishing boat had cruised past—probably on its way to shelter from the storm.

Caleb was showing the men where the ferry would be at the time they would blow the car bomb. They would use a jet ski to pick up the one who sets the bomb. "Who's the best swimmer?" Caleb asked them.

They looked at each other and shrugged. "Tommy here grew up in Sandpoint. Right on the lake."

"Good. Then you'll set the bomb and jump off the stern." Caleb gave the man a hard stare. "Not in that order. The bomb will be on a timer."

The man looked relieved.

That was good, Caleb thought. These fuckers weren't looking for a one-way ticket. Without the four of them knowing it, Caleb had gotten plenty of information on each of them. Colleges attended. Hometowns. He was better than he thought at this shit. His friend Pat started to catch on, and would smile when they heard something new about the men. Any longer and they'd have a complete history. Good thing Caleb had insisted on them bugging the cabin.

Badger sat somewhat nervously next to the woman, Donna. He whispered something into her ear and then got up. Stopping next to Pat, he said, "Let's see the night vision goggles." He had his hand out until Pat slid the strap from around his neck and handed him the NVGs. When Badger got them, he shifted his head to Donna, who followed him up the steps.

Caleb and Pat shared a stare. Something wasn't right.

◆

Topside, Badger and Donna moved toward the

stern. He put the goggles to his eyes and scanned the horizon. It was nearly impossible to see anything with the wind rocking the boat like that.

"What's wrong?" she asked him.

There. He finally saw the fishing boat, its nose pointed right at them, moving slowly toward their location. The boat was now within a hundred yards. Two people aboard.

"Get in the raft," Badger ordered.

"What's wrong?"

"Get in the fuckin' raft. Now! It's a set-up."

They both scrambled into the small raft and Donna untied them, almost falling into the dark water. Badger quickly went with the waves toward shore, the electric motor making no sound whatsoever against the background of the howling wind.

◆

Tony now had the fishing boat tacking toward the stern of Virtue's boat, the occasional heavier wave nearly capsizing them. But at least they were moving faster, making swifter progress toward their target.

When the stern of Virtue's boat got closer, Tony let up on the throttle and the boat slowly bumped into a rubber bar. Before Carrie could react, Panzer shoved around her and jumped to the back of the larger craft. Carrie recovered and lashed a bow rope around a cleat.

After Carrie scrambled to Virtue's boat and tried her best to hold the boat against the strong tide, Tony made his way to the bow and, almost falling into the ocean, he shuffled aboard next to her.

Tony glanced about the boat, looking for Panzer, but the dog wasn't there. They pulled their guns and moved forward to the cabin door.

There was only one way in or out. Surprise was on their side.

Before they could take another step, a flash of light broke the darkness, followed by a resounding crack from a gun.

The bullet caught Tony on the top of his left shoulder, three inches from his face. He ducked behind the cabin structure, his heart pounding.

Tony heard a growl and scuffling. A man screamed to get the damn beast off of him.

Another gun shot. Carrie, kneeling beside Tony, grabbed onto his arm.

Silence.

Tony yelled, "Hold." Then "Schlafen." He paused for a moment, so as not to confuse Panzer, and then said, "If you killed my dog, you're dead." He put the NVGs to his head and wished now he had a laser sight on his .40 cal auto.

The cabin door creaked open. "Tone, that you?"

It was Caleb Hatfield.

"Is it secure there?" Tony asked.

"Hell yeah."

"Then stay there and keep your head down."

Another bullet broke the night. Passed by between them.

Tony and Carrie ducked down further.

They were pinned there with no place to move. Other than back. That gave Tony an idea. He whispered into Carrie's ear that he was taking the boat around to the front. They'd have the advantage then.

Quietly Tony got back into the Lund boat, untied the bow, and then powered up the quiet electric motor. But now he had a problem. With one hand on the throttle and the other trying to hold the NVGs, he would have to put his gun down. First get Panzer, he thought, and then worry about those four assholes. As a compromise, he shoved his gun tightly between his knees.

Moments later, the Lund was cruising around to the front of Virtue's boat. Tony immediately saw two men crouched along the forward rail. He guessed Panzer was laying flat against the forward deck.

Waves crashed against the side of Tony's boat, nearly rocking him from his seat. He recovered and looked through the NVGs again. Where were the other two men?

Gunfire from the stern. Carrie shooting.

Followed by two shots. There they were. One on each side of the cabin structure.

Tony moved the Lund around to the bow of Virtue's boat. If they found out he was there, he'd be an easy target. He had to turn this around to his favor. How?

He was shivering now with the cold rain when the idea came to him. But that thought was shattered when the half moon suddenly appeared, exposing him to them, yet also silhouetting them against the hull. It could still work.

The Lund was now some fifty yards away from Virtue's boat, the wind and waves having pulled

Tony away in a hurry. He had no choice. He had to
start the main Merc motor or he would soon smash
into shore.

Cranking over the motor, nothing happened. Shit!

He tried again. It whirred but didn't flip over.
Damn it! Sitting at the wheel around two-thirds of the
way back, Tony thought about going to the motor and
priming more gas into it. But he didn't have time. It
had to turn over. In the moonlight he could see the
trees along the shore closing in. "Turn over you black
devil," he growled under his breath.

The motor started and Tony slowly moved away
from the shore toward Virtue's boat. He had drifted
nearly a hundred yards. Not a problem. The gunfire
from the boat was the problem.

He increased speed toward Virtue's boat. The
clouds covered the moon again and the wind picked
up, driving rain like shards of steel into Tony's face.

Would Panzer hear him? With his ears. . .damn
straight.

Thirty yards out.

In a normal voice, Tony said, "Panzer. . .come."

Seconds later, Tony saw a black flash fly overboard, followed by a heavy splash.

A man appeared at the rail and shot twice toward
the water. Tony had his gun up from his knees in a
second and shot twice. The man disappeared.

Slowing the boat to idle, Tony turned the wheel,
which swiveled the boat sideways. Then he shoved
his gun into its holster and reached down for Panzer.

"Good boy," he said to the dog at the side of the
boat. He grabbed for the dog's collar, but with him

pulling on the dog the boat nearly capsized. He'd have to move to the stern. "Come along, Panzer."

The dog was paddling away with all its might, rising and falling with the waves, as Tony pulled him toward the motor. There was a small ledge there and Tony pulled Panzer's paws onto it. With both of their strength, the dog scrambled aboard and then shook off the water.

Back to the wheel. Tony sat into the chair and looked back at Virtue's boat. They had drifted back again. A good thing, Tony thought.

More gunshots on the boat from the front and the back. He sure as hell hoped Carrie had enough extra magazines.

Panzer, his tongue out and panting, was sitting now at Tony's feet. "Schlafen da," Tony said, and his dog immediately lay at his feet.

This is bullshit. Tony cranked the wheel around and powered up the motor. Moving adjacent to Virtue's boat, Tony snapped the wheel around and shoved the throttle to the max.

Pulling out his gun, Tony started shooting and didn't stop until the Lund rammed into the port bow of Virtue's vessel.

The great collision hurtled Tony from his seat and against the wheel console, his gun flying from his wet grip. Tony rolled to the side and landed on the deck. He scrambled about with his hands searching for his gun.

A blast behind him stopped Tony. He rolled to his side and saw the man at the rail pointing his gun at him.

A shot rang out from the stern, dropping the gunman.

"Tony?" came Carrie's voice. "You all right?"

By now the Lund had drifted away from Virtue's boat.

Tony felt for any wounds, but, other than the cold, which had been held back somewhat by adrenalin, he felt pretty good.

Then came the spotlight. That followed immediately by a large caliber machine gun fire across the bow of Virtue's boat. Tony knew that sound. . .a .50 caliber.

CHAPTER 22

Tony was able to tie up the Lund to the back of Virtue's boat again. He and Panzer came aboard and found Carrie Jones where he had left her.

By now, the Navy Mark V was alongside the starboard side, one man at the bow directing his .50 cal at the bow of Virtue's boat while four men in black hurried aboard, their MP5s leading the way. Three men went forward and one came to Tony and Carrie.

"Agent Jones?" the large black-faced man said.

Carrie holstered her gun. "Yeah."

The man turned toward Tony. "Tony Caruso?"

"Yeah. What the hell took ya?"

"Looks like we got here just in time to save your Ordy ass," the man said.

"Ordy?" Carrie said.

"Ordnance," Tony explained.

She nodded.

Another of the SEAL team came around to them from the bow and said, "Sir, there's only one who hasn't been shot." He looked down at Panzer and added, "And he's pretty torn up by a dog. Said his dick was damn near off. He's in a bad way."

"The others?" The SEAL team leader asked.

"Two dead. One will live."

Tony said, "What about the woman? And does one of them have a skunk head?"

The sailor shook his head. "No, sir. No woman or any man like that."

With that, Tony hurried into the cabin and down the steps. Somewhat startled and standing in the back of the cabin, the look on the faces of Caleb Hatfield and Pat Virtue changed from surprise to relief in a matter of seconds.

"Where the fuck are they?" Tony yelled.

Neither of them said a thing for a long minute.

"We needed to let them escape," Caleb finally said.

Carrie had already started up the stairs, but now came down onto the main deck, listening intently.

Virtue broke the silence. "We were told to let them go."

Tony's mind started to reel. "Let me guess. You guys tagged them somehow."

Carrie, dripping wet, water dropping to the deck, holstered her gun, accepted a towel from Virtue, and started wiping her face. Tony thought hard about what had just happened.

"You set us up," Tony said. "To make these guys think we were breaking up the show. But you let the two main players escape and head back to Seattle."

Carrie said, "Right. Then you track them back to their friends."

"Exactly," Caleb said. "There was no other way.

We were supposed to teach the men how to set the bombs. But we guessed our lives wouldn't be worth a damn once they had the info."

Tony smiled and said, "But you didn't teach them right."

Caleb shrugged. "Hell no. Like I could give them more than twenty years of knowledge in one evening. We planted the GPS trackers on Badger and this Donna woman. We also gave each man a kit to take back and train on their own. Like I said, there was no other way. Each cell is separate. These were only the leaders of each cell. We needed to know all the players, down to Joe Worker Bee."

Carrie set a towel on the bench and sat down, her extreme shiver calming down now. "Who are you working for?"

"I can't say," Caleb said.

"I'm a special agent with the FBI," she reminded him.

Caleb looked at Tony for help.

"You need her," Tony said. "There was that problem at the forest service fire." The accidental murder had now become a problem.

"That was an accident," Pat said. "There was no way to know that guy would be there."

"Still. . . ," Carrie said, her eyes nondescript.

Virtue ran his fingers through his hair. "This is bullshit. We were just following orders."

"Whose orders?" Carrie said.

Tony glared at his friend. "Caleb?"

Caleb hesitated and then said, "We're working for the NSA. I told you that."

Now Carrie glared at Tony. "You did?"

"We didn't have a whole lot of time to discuss the matter," Tony said. "Remember. . .a group of FBI agents, along with some Navy Base Security pushed us from that carrier. Caleb had just mentioned the NSA, but didn't have time to elaborate."

There was silence for a while until Tony realized he had forgotten about Panzer. He grabbed a towel, hurried up the steps and opened the door. Tony grasped Panzer's collar and led him down the stairs. Then he put the towel over the black fur just before the dog shook violently, extricating the rain into the towel.

"Holy shit!" Pat said. "Fucker looks like a bear."

Caleb laughed. "Shit. Panzer eats bear for lunch."

The dog moved over and sniffed Caleb, who reached down to the wet dog and scratched him under the chin. "You remember me, Panzer?"

The NSA team leader came down into the cabin, his eyes barely visible behind the face paint. "Which one is Commander Caleb Hatfield?"

"That's me."

"Sir, we have the situation topside sanitized. The admiral says he wants the tapes from down here, and for you to come along with us." He turned to Virtue, who was sitting somewhat subdued on the bench, and said. "This your boat, sir?"

Virtue nodded.

"You got a little damage, but she'll make it back to Seabeck."

"Can we follow you back as far as Bangor?"

"Negative, sir," the NSA leader said. "We have to haul ass. Get the one some medical help and interrogate the other. What happened to the skunk-headed dude and the woman?"

Caleb said, "We think they took the inflatable to shore just before all hell broke loose."

"Is he armed?"

"Yes."

Tony glanced down at Panzer. "Let my dog get him."

"They've got a helluva lead," Caleb said.

"Yeah, well Panzer is faster."

Carrie Jones stepped forward and said, "Let's go. Let's see what kind of nose that dog of yours has."

Tony glanced about. "Got some NVGs for special agent Jones?"

Pat shook his head. "That skunk fucker took 'em."

"A flashlight then," Carrie said.

Virtue pulled out a five-battery Mag Lite and handed it to Carrie.

Tony started to go and stopped. He brought Panzer around the cabin, having him sniff anything and everything, hoping he'd hit on something once they got out onto land. Then he and Carrie went back to the Lund and Tony fired up the motor. It started the first time.

As they got closer to shore, the other boats in the bay turned and head toward the inlet, the Navy Mark V flying at top speed and Virtue's boat trying like hell to keep up.

Carrie had the NVGs in the bow, Panzer sitting to her left. "There's the raft," she said, pointing toward shore.

Tony slowed the Lund and found a spot to bring the

bow ashore. Seconds later, Carrie had the boat tied to a tree and Tony had Panzer sniffing the inside of the rubber raft. The dog was going nuts with excitement.

Panzer was not trained specifically to search for suspects, his training in explosives and drugs, but he had done it quite successfully for Tony in the past. Tony pulled a six-foot leash from his pocket and snapped it to Panzer's collar.

"Won't that slow him down," Carrie asked, her words a whisper.

"Yeah. But if I let him run, I'm not sure we'll ever catch up with him." Panzer sat at the ready, his eyes looking up to Tony for direction. "Suchen," Tony said authoritatively.

The dog headed off immediately, pulling against the thick nylon leash.

"What you tell him?" Carrie asked, her steps right on Tony's heels.

"Search in German."

"I love it," she said. "A bi-lingual dog. And most humans can't even understand one."

Panzer rushed through the thick cedars and pines, Tony having a difficult time holding him back. It was evident the dog wanted to move much quicker, but Panzer didn't bark when he searched. He and Carrie would have no idea which direction Panzer was leading them. Tony tried to remember the geography of this area of northern Kitsap, but he wasn't entirely sure of what lay ahead. He knew there was a highway running right down the center on the peninsula all the way to Hansville and Point No Point, and another that cut off to Little Boston. But he was sure they had to be a bit south of there. The main Hansville road would be a mile or two to the east. Yet they had one advantage over their targets. . .Panzer.

"There's a road perhaps a mile ahead," Tony said. "If they get to that, they could flag down a car and be back to Kingston in twenty minutes."

"You think that guy will head for the road?" Carrie asked.

"I would. No other place to go without a boat. The peninsula is only about four or five miles wide at this point." He had to let Panzer go. There was no other way.

Tony pulled the dog to a stop. But Panzer didn't sit, he just gave Tony a confused look. He unclipped the leash and pointed to the woods. "Suchen. Schnell."

The dog beat tracks through the woods at full speed.

"Why'd you change your mind?" she asked him.

"When he catches up with them, which he will, I think we'll hear about it." Tony headed off through the woods, the flashlight directing his way.

Ten minutes later a shot echoed through the forest, stopping Tony and Carrie cold in their tracks. As they listened, they could hear both a man screaming and a woman yelling. They were closer than Tony thought. He ran now, hoping like hell his dog had not taken a bullet. He was aware of Carrie trying to keep up behind him. As the sound of snarling dog and human screaming got closer, Tony pulled his gun from its holster.

Branches whipped across Tony's face as he ran through the thick forest, his feet soggy from the marshy bottom and his entire body soaking wet from the rain coming down through the trees.

He could feel Carrie keeping up with him.

Panzer had stopped growling, and now only a lone woman sobbed and plead.

Seconds later Tony emerged from the forest onto a paved county road. He pointed his flashlight at the scene alongside the near shoulder. A woman stood back a few feet from Panzer, who had his mouth around the neck of the skunk-headed puke. They all seemed frozen in time.

Carrie had her gun out and pointed at the woman and then swiftly had her in cuffs face down on the gravel.

Tony looked around for the gun, but couldn't see it. The man at the mercy of his dog had his hands spread out at his sides, his fingers taping lightly against the dirt. He couldn't say a word if he wanted to.

Shoving his gun in its holster, Tony patted Panzer on his neck. "Gut Arbeit, Panzer. Frei." The dog let go and then shoved its nose under the man's back until the guy rolled over onto his side, revealing the gun. "Roll over onto your belly," Tony said. The man lay on his side, not moving. "I'm talking to you, dumbass." Tony kicked the gun a few feet away and then planted his shoe into the guy's butt until he lay on his stomach.

"Thought you were talking to your dog," Badger said.

"Yeah, right."

Carrie got on her cell phone and called in their situation, asking for the locals to transport. Then she secured the gun, zip-strapped the man, and searched both of them for ID and anything else of interest. The man known only as Badger was really Wesley Wilson with a Mercer Island address. The woman also had a Mercer Island address. They lived less than a mile apart.

Knowing it would take some time for the local cops to arrive, Tony convinced Carrie to let him have a talk with the man. Alone. At first the man was not too forthright with information. It wasn't until Tony had Panzer sit a foot from Wilson, teeth bared, that he decided to talk. Coercion? Maybe. But method had given way to results. But then Tony didn't work for the FBI or any other federal agency. They needed to know what else was out there. What they found was more than they had expected.

Tony leaned in, grabbed the man by his long hair, and whispered into his ear, "Keep your mouth shut about this until morning. You understand?"

The man nodded, his eyes full of fear.

The local highway patrol was the first to arrive, fol-lowed by two Kitsap County cruisers. Carrie was tight-lipped about who they had or what it was all about—simply stating national security implications. Tony noticed she had an extremely authoritarian ease about her. Remarkable, considering all that had hap-pened in the past few hours.

They all traveled back to the Kitsap County Jail, Panzer riding in the back seat next to a frightened-looking Wesley Wilson.

Without waiting for booking, Tony and Carrie got out of there.

CHAPTER 23

Driving from Kitsap County to the north Seattle suburb of Edmonds it could take anywhere from two hours to never during rush hour, or thirty minutes by ferry from Kingston. After having a deputy drive them to Tony's truck, they made it to the Kingston Ferry Terminal just in time to make the 11:10 p.m. crossing.

Neither Carrie or Tony said much on the crossing, having stayed in the truck with Panzer sleeping in the back. It wasn't until they rolled down the ramp and drove down the quiet streets of Edmonds that they started to talk about what they would do.

"You've been quiet," Carrie said. "What's the matter?"

Tony hunched his shoulders. "You think you know someone. But how much do we really know about anyone?" He watched the GPS navigation on the portable unit on his dash, telling him to turn right at the next block ahead.

"Is that why you never married?" She looked away after her question. "I'm sorry."

"No. You're probably right. I used the Navy as an excuse for so many years. But it was hard to establish a lasting relationship when I was out to sea so much for more than twenty years. And even if you did establish something, I saw far too many marriages self destruct during all of those deployments."

"I understand," she muttered. "It's three blocks ahead."

"You've been there?"

"A barbeque about a month ago."

"He used to live in a little three bedroom ranch in Kirkland. He's moving up. This is a nice neighborhood."

"Yeah. Pull over here."

Tony pulled the truck to the curb. The dark, deserted streets were lined with tall maples and oaks, which swayed with a stiff breeze. The houses looked like turn of the last century—two story Victorian, and even in the darkness quite well maintained.

He turned off the truck. "How you want to play this?" Tony asked her. He could tell she was struggling with the duty at hand.

"You need to let me do my job," she said.

"I won't let you do this on your own," Tony insisted. "Remember, I also knew Bob. We didn't always get along, but he didn't deserve what he got."

She considered his words.

"I'll just cover your back," he assured her.

She smiled. "All right. Bring that bear of yours."

They got out quietly, still a block from the house, and Tony let Panzer out. She gave him a two-way ear piece so they could be in radio contact, using a scrambled military frequency. They both checked their guns to make sure they had full magazines, and then slowly walked up the sidewalk toward the house. Tony would go around to the back and Carrie would simply knock on the front door. A simple plan.

As they got closer, Tony pulled his gun and made his way around to the back of the house. He set himself up along the edge of the house with a clear shot of the back steps.

"In place?" she asked.

"Roger."

"Going in."

He could hear a faint knock around the front, followed by Carrie asking to open the door. She needed to talk. Sounding distressed, not like an official FBI agent.

Pop. . .Pop. . .Pop!

"Crap!" Tony screamed softly. Into the mic, he said, "Carrie. Talk to me."

Nothing.

"Carrie!" Should he go to her or hold tight? He had only a slit second to decide, but then heard footfalls in the house so he held tight.

Seconds later the door burst open and a dark figure scooted down the steps.

Tony yelled, "Stop! Federal Agent!"

The man, at the bottom of the steps now, raised his gun at Tony, but Tony shot first. Twice. The first bullet smashed through the man's right shoulder, making that arm with the gun go limp. The second bullet clipped the man's right ear, the percussion dropping the man to the sidewalk.

Panzer pounced into action and was on top of the man in seconds, his jaw grasping the man's right arm and pulling him toward the damp grass.

Tony kicked the man's gun aside as the guy screamed in pain. Into the mic, he said, "Carrie, you all right?"

"Yeah, I'll live," she said, as she came up behind him, her gun drawn. "First time I've been shot in the Kevlar. Wow. You gonna let your dog eat him or what?"

"Oh. Panzer. . .halt." The dog stopped and looked at Tony. "Sitzen." Panzer sat.

The man started to sob now, his hand putting pressure on his broken shoulder.

Carrie pulled her cuffs, but Tony said, "Let me talk with him first."

She nodded and handed the cuffs to Tony. "Somebody had to have called the local cops. I'll head them off out front. Call it in so they don't come guns blazing."

Tony knelt down to the man. "Why'd you do it, Jim?"

FBI Special Agent Jim Pratt continued to sob. "I had to," he finally sniveled. Bob was getting too close. He would have turned me in."

"But why'd you get caught up with these people in the first place?" Tony pressed.

"I'm sorry Tony," Jim said. "I didn't mean for it to go this far. They promised nobody would get hurt. They were just trying to save the environment."

Tony shook his head. "They were planning to do a lot more than that, Jim. They were going to bomb bridges, bomb a major ferry."

Jim shook his head. "No, that's not true," he pled. "Not true."

"Onto your stomach, Jim."

"You have no authority, Tony."

Aiming his gun at the man's head, Tony said, "I have the gun. That's all I need. Now roll over. You'll need to get used to that."

Jim Pratt did as he was told and Tony cuffed his hands behind his back.

The next hour was spent with Carrie explaining to the local police that the FBI had jurisdiction. That this rogue agent was in her custody, wanted for murder and conspiracy to commit murder, along with countless charges of terrorism and maybe treason. Tony tried his best to hang back and stay out of it.

♦

Special Agent Carrie Jones lived in a one-story house, nestled among tall firs and cedars, in Lake Forest Park, a northern Seattle suburb a half mile north of the northern tip of Lake Washington. She and Tony had gotten there at nearly three a.m. after dropping Jim Pratt at the local hospital, exhausted and still in their same clothes, which had turned from soaking wet to merely damp and smelly. They had stripped down, thrown the clothes in the washer while they drank a beer, and then gone to bed once the clothes got to the dryer.

Now, rolling in on noon, Tony woke and rolled to his side. Panzer was on a blanket Carrie had found for him the night before, but Carrie was nowhere in sight. He could hear noises out in the kitchen, though. His stomach growled at that moment. He lifted the covers and realized he was naked. Then he remembered throwing the clothes in the washer the night before. Looking around, he saw his clothes folded and stacked on the dresser next to his gun and holster.

He got up and dressed, Panzer still not moving.

When he got into the kitchen, Carrie was sipping coffee. She poured Tony a cup and they both took a seat at the kitchen table.

"How long you been up?" Tony asked her.

"About an hour. Panzer snores."

"Yeah, he does. Thanks for the clothes."

"No problem." She stared at him and then said, "I let Panzer out for a pee break when I got up."

"Thanks. He's sleeping again."

They stared at each other for a while, sipping coffee.

"I called the office," she said. "They said Bob was killed instantly. Probably didn't know what hit him."

Although Tony and Bob McCallum had not gotten along, it was still difficult to hear he had been shot and killed. He didn't deserve that.

"How's our friend Jim Pratt doing?" Tony asked.

She shrugged. "Had to go through surgery for his shoulder and a plastic surgeon was able to sew up most of his ear. Were you aiming for that?"

"I don't know. I aimed for the shoulder first. Hit that mark. Second shot just went off. I didn't think there was any reason to let him take the easy way out.

Prison will be much more fun for him. Especially as an FBI agent." Truth is, he had aimed for the center of the man's face, but in the excitement had pulled his shot. But Carrie didn't need to know that.

"What happens now?"

"You're asking me?"

"Well, I know what happens with the case. We get all kinds of crap from Washington, a new boss. Probably some hard ass. Everyone in the office gets hooked up to a lie detector. Bunch of bullshit."

But that's not what she was asking him, and he knew it. Truth is, he didn't know where they stood. "And with us?" he asked.

"That's what I was asking you."

He reached across the table and took her hand. "I think we still have some discovery."

She smiled. "Yeah. I agree."

CHAPTER 24

Tony pulled into the long driveway of Caleb Hatfield's house in Port Orchard. It had been two days since he saw his old friend. He let Panzer out of the back and let the dog run around the front yard.

Caleb came out the front door looking totally changed. His pony tail had been cut and replaced with a flat top. He wore a gray Navy T-shirt and jeans, looking like he was ready for liberty.

The two of them shook hands and then embraced.

"Thanks," Caleb said. "I didn't want you to get involved, but I'm glad you did."

"No problem. Ordies need to stick together."

"You got that shit right. If you ain't ordnance, you ain't shit." The mantra of Navy Ordnancemen for decades.

"I hear the Feds won't mess with you for the guy who died at the forest service office," Tony said. "That's nice of them, considering you probably saved thousands of lives by catching those dirtbags."

"Hey, the NSA could have hung me out to dry. As

you know, they aren't supposed to operate stateside."

"About time they do, though."

"Your FBI friend helped also. You gonna keep in touch with her?"

Tony shrugged. "Don't know. We'll see if our schedules match."

"You've got to make time, Tony."

He knew that. "Did Mary get to Dry Dock all right?"

"Yeah, I drove her to the rehab center in Port Angeles last night. Supposed to be the Betty Ford of the Northwest."

"That's great, Caleb. I'm sure she'll do great." He hesitated, unsure what else to say.

"Any word on the other men in the cells?" Caleb asked.

"They've been rounding them up the last couple of days. As far as I know they've got them all. And they've been talking. Most have been part of the EDL for years, pulling off all kinds of crap for a decade."

"The FBI should clear a lot of cases."

"Why would an ex-dot.com multi-millionare decide it was a good idea to blow shit up?" Caleb asked.

"I think he was just bored. He made his first million while still in college at UW. He was a math major with a theatre minor. Had a great idea going into computers at just the right time, started his website, which grew from his frat house basement into a hundred and fifty employees in two years. Then a bigger dot.com bought him out for half a billion and he's been growing his hair and beard and playing the socialite by day and the enviro-wacko by night. Strange combo."

"Well, he'll be taking it from behind from now on. You did good, bro."

They both smiled.

Caleb said, "What about that rogue FBI agent. What made him go crazy?"

Tony thought about that. He had known Jim Pratt to be a quiet, gentle man. "I don't know for sure. He was a good guy. But his wife left him recently, and would be taking half of his FBI retirement. He has two kids in college. Must have needed the money. Bob must have figured out that Jim was the mole, feeding the EDL tips on when the Feds were moving in on them. A lot of money flowed from that skunk-headed bastard to Jim in an offshore account.

They both watched Panzer run along the edge of Caleb's yard.

"Now what?" Caleb asked.

"I say you take me fishing."

"Can't beat that with a stick."

They embraced again.

MAY 1 2 2008

9 781930 486737